PRAISE FOR *WE ARE HAPPY, WE ARE DOOMED*

"Fawver's latest collection is unsettling not only for the strangeness of his imagination but for the way in which he can move deeply into odd and uncanny territories that are still deeply haunted by the politics of our current moment. At the heart of *We are Happy, We are Doomed* are fractured and confused communities, struggling to pursue a way forward while still not entirely sure what has traumatized them. A powerful and resonant collection by a nimble writer and thinker."

— Brian Evenson, author of *Last Days*

"Kurt Fawver is one of the most innovative and unique voices to emerge in weird fiction in the last decade, and his collection, *We are Happy, We are Doomed,* is proof why. These dark and strange tales contain foreboding landscapes, unusual formats, and a pervading sense of dread that creeps up on you and never quite lets you go. Highly recommended."

— Gwendolyn Kiste, Bram Stoker Award-winning author of *The Rust Maidens* and *Reluctant Immortals*

"Delightfully acerbic, poetically strange, *We are Happy, We are Doomed* builds upon bedrock weird fiction influences to rise as its own dark island. If we're talking about Thomas Ligotti and Michael Cisco, we need to be talking about Kurt Fawver."

— Laird Barron, author of *Swift to Chase*

"These stories are reminiscent of ethnographies, oral histories exploring the darkest regions of existence, and the remarkably diverse manifestations alternate worlds may take. Here Fawver proves once more that he's capable of evoking not only mordant terror, but profound humanity coupled with scathing socio-political awareness, accentuated by profound philosophical insight—often in the same story. There's nothing quite like it out there; Fawver's creations are unique. I've no idea how he does it, but finishing this collection made me feel as if I were sinking into the molasses-thick dark matter that permeates the universe. Like some Fortean academic of dread, *We are Happy, We are Doomed* reads as a hortative colloquy building deliriously until the lecture theater dims and you're no longer certain what constitutes reality, much less what it means to be human. Fawver is an absolute master of the strange fable."

— Christopher Slatsky, author of
The Immeasurable Corpse of Nature

"*We are Happy, We are Doomed* demonstrates Fawver's continued transformation into one of the most interesting writers in modern weird fiction. His singular vision crosses back and forth across the thin boundary separating the absurd from the horrific, creating amalgamations that are as bizarre as they are unnerving. Kurt Fawver has staked a claim in the genre that's all his own."

— Simon Strantzas, author of
Nothing is Everything

"Kurt Fawver traffics in dark allegories, deeply strange fables, and the boldly outré. He's a true original, a treasure, and *We are Happy, We are Doomed* is a showcase for some of his finest work to date."

— Matthew M. Bartlett, author of
Gateways to Abomination

"Small towns, apocalypses, deformed bodies, and sensory oddities wind through this strong collection of weird fiction from Fawver ...[H]is ideas are highly original and memorable."

— *Publisher's Weekly*

We are Happy, We are Doomed

Kurt Fawver

Grimscribe Press

New Orleans, Louisiana

Cover and interior art by Harry o. Morris

Cover design by Jon Padgett

Published by

Grimscribe Press
New Orleans, LA
USA

grimscribepress.com

CONTENTS

The Bleeding Maze: A Visitor's Guide

I WANT TO TELL you about the bleeding maze at the center of our town. People who aren't from around here don't know anything about it. It's not referenced on any website or in any travel book, and most of us like it that way. We don't share the knowledge of its existence with just anyone because it's a very personal thing, the maze. We all have longstanding relationships with it that began at a young age. See, when kids in our town turn eighteen, we force them to enter it, like our parents did to us and their parents did to them. Inside the maze we have unique experiences, formative experiences. Most of us return from these experiences just fine—or, fine enough, at least. The others... well, I'll get to them later. The point here is: the maze underscores our lives. You might even say that, in several important ways, it's inescapable.

Now, I don't want you to think our town and the people in it are anything out of the ordinary. They're not. Our town is economically middling, and our townsfolk are generally content in their strife, just like in most places around the world. We have no special talents or knowledge, no outstanding attractions that differentiate us from a million other forgettable locales. The maze just happens to be *here*. It could be anywhere else, and it would still function the same way. For all I know, everyone has a maze in their town and doesn't tell anyone else for the same reasons we give. In fact, maybe, right now, you're thinking, "I already know about the maze. I bet yours isn't any different from ours." But, then again, maybe not. Maybe there's only one maze, our maze, *the* maze, ever ready for new entrants and ever ready to spit them out.

So, assuming you don't know about it already, you're probably wondering, "What *is* this maze, exactly?" As best as I can explain, it's one of those traditional labyrinth deals, I guess, like in the Ancient Greek mythological sense. It's pentagonal, with a perimeter of over three miles on last measurement, but it used to be smaller. Much smaller. Town records show that it's grown more expansive over the years, swallowing up and demolishing homes and businesses in its path. No one admits to having built new corridors or walls, so we can't explain the increasing size deviations, nor do we try. Even though it may one day consume the entire town, it's really in everyone's interest not to think about certain facts of the maze. We all sleep better that way.

Structurally, the maze is comprised of cold, gray stone polished ice-smooth. At least, we think it's stone. There's every possibility that it's not. After all, the walls of the maze take no damage even when battered with hammers, chisels, and axes. Standing over nine feet high, they have never been scaled by any climbers, either. Anyone who tries slips off and comes crashing back to earth, as if the stone actively resists attempts at mastery. Rock collectors among us say the "stone" of the maze walls seems like granite, except for its abnormal hardness. That hardness is really the lesser of its abnormalities, though, as it's also infused with something our local mineral and stone enthusiasts can't come close to identifying: dark red flecks impenetrable as the rest of the stone one minute and permeable the next. When these flecks become permeable, a syrupy liquid of the same dark red color seeps from them and coats the maze. There's no mistaking that the liquid is anything other than blood.

A few months ago, the senior biology teacher in our high school decided to collect a sample of the blood and send it off to a lab for genetic testing. The lab responded with a letter that explained how the tests couldn't be completed because the blood seemed to be from not one discrete individual, but an amalgam of people. However, it could not estimate how many people with any certainty, as every strand of DNA examined appeared to be of a separate origin from the others. What meaning this result provided is unclear, but it made us extremely uneasy. We resolved to never inspect the blood that closely again.

How long the maze has been here is impossible to say. Some of us believe it's always been where it is, ageless and indestructible, a universal constant of a sort. Some of us believe it was built when the first people arrived here, however many hundreds or thousands or hundreds of thousands of years ago that might have been. And some of us believe it's part of a conspiracy, that it's a newer structure built to look ancient, that our parents and their parents never actually stumbled through the maze but claim they did so that we would go in and, later, send our own children to do the same. Regardless of the truth of its age, everyone in our town accepts that it's part of a scheme much greater and much more complex than our individual lives or even the life of the town.

Navigating the maze is difficult due to its layout and its size. It has, seemingly, four entry points, but we know that these are really just a paired set of entrances and exits. How do we know? Because the maze calls to us. Certain kinds of people always gravitate toward a particular entrance. No one ever enters an exit. Some families try to coach their children to choose one entrance over the other, but, in the end, no one is ever entirely sure who will walk which side of the maze. Families who coach their kids to choose a particular path are often distressed when their child emerges from the exit that's paired with the opposite entrance. Some of those families see this emergence as a conscious betrayal of their advice, their teaching. Others are merely disappointed in the choices their children made within the maze that brought them to an alternative end. A few among these families even stop talking to their children altogether if they return from the "wrong" exit. As far as we can tell, though, there is little variation in the two paths. They both twist and turn in bizarre, chaotic patterns. They both result in journeys of indeterminate duration. They both lead to exits that stand no more than ten feet from one another. And, at the end, everyone who passes through either one returns soaked in blood, if, indeed, they return.

What happens to us inside the maze is that which I suppose sociologists might call a coming of age ritual, though it's a distinctly different experience for everyone. Some of us try to run through as quickly as our legs and lungs will allow; some of us attempt to stroll or make a game of it; some of us hope to camp out and spend the night. It doesn't matter the tactic used because the maze itself determines how long our journeys take.

For many, traversing the maze is a process of mere hours. Those who fall into this category usually arrive with compasses and coordinates and GPS systems all set to guide them. They map out their trajectory with help from older family and friends who've already wandered the maze and can recall bits and pieces of it. They know where they're headed—or they believe they do, at least—and they make every effort to stick to their plans. The ones who are successful in this endeavor return slicked in gore, as it's impossible to roam the maze's tight alleyways without rubbing up against shed blood, but none the worse for wear. In truth, many of these teens will find themselves energized by the trek and become the maze's most vocal supporters in their adult years. They find nothing unusual or upsetting inside the maze, yet something in these quick and easy finishers seems missing. They shake hands too firmly, speak their opinions too loudly, and never, ever, apologize to anyone for any reason. They take comfort in their self-certainty and general assuredness, rarely admitting a need for anything or anyone beyond their gods, especially the one they worship in the mirror. When you meet one of these people, you'll be left with either a chill in your heart or a thorn in your mind, and you'll be just as happy to never meet with them again. So it is with the easy finishers.

In contrast, the teens who plan and map and use all the resources in the world but still struggle to locate an exit have stories to tell—stories that betoken both the depth of the teens themselves and the strangeness of the maze, stories similar to those who lack such supplies and preparation.

Here I must impress upon you the glaring fact that not every family in our town has the means to outfit their children for the maze. Some are in want of the knowledge required to properly lay out a guiding route. Some possess no funds to purchase supplies. Others simply don't care what their kids do within the maze or if they find a way back out. For the teens in these families, the maze is a shifting, confusing thing, beset with hardships and taking many days, weeks, months, or even years to finish. They return through guile, intelligence, fortitude, strength, and luck. Many are worn to a nub in body and spirit. Some are hardened to steel. A few never re-emerge from the maze at all. As I said, though, like the failed planners, the less prepared among us who *do* come back usually return with remarkable stories to tell, each one unique in its intricacies. Let me give you some examples.

One of our oldest residents, Theresa Chubb, walked into the maze as a young woman with only a single canteen of water, but exited a week later with two satchels full of jewel-encrusted human skulls. As she explained upon returning, "In the maze, I met a peculiar man without any features I can recall. He was neither handsome nor homely, short nor tall, stocky nor thin. His skin wasn't black or white or brown or red or yellow, but somehow all those colors at once. He wore a threadbare gray suit and carried with him a pair of shiny silver sickles. He told me he could lead me through the maze, but that I had to help him first. He said the maze was infested with parasites and that it was his job to get rid of them. He asked if I could sing to lure them out of hiding. He said they loved to hear young women and young men. Well, that made my decision for me. He called me a woman rather than a girl or a lady. No one had ever done that before, so I said I could help him. And I did. I sang all the showtunes I knew, and the man led me through the maze.

"At first, I didn't think we'd see anything. I thought the man was a little crazy, maybe. But as we kept moving, I heard rustling around us. I was scared by it. I should've been scared by the peculiar man and his sickles, I suppose, but it was the rustling that didn't seem right to me. I couldn't understand where it was coming from. Well, the rustling grew louder, and the walls of the maze started bleeding, and I heard something like an explosion. That's when the gilded men appeared. Two of them, to be exact, fully naked. Their skin glinted in the sun, and their eyes had no color other than gold. They smiled at me, and their teeth, pointed like a shark's, glittered red and blue and green. They began stalking toward me, and I worried what their smiles meant.

"The peculiar man, though, moved in a flash. It was almost as if he popped in and out of space. He was in front of me one second, then behind the gilded men the next, then slashing his sickle across their necks from right in front of them the next. Three seconds and their heads rolled off their bodies. That's all it took. They bled gold, but the peculiar man had no interest in the blood.

Instead, he carved the shiny skin from the heads and rolled it into scrolls like parchment, then pulled a satchel from thin air and placed the heads inside it. He handed me the bag and said I should take the heads back with me, that they'd be worth more where I was going.

"We spent a long time repeating the same sequence. Walking, singing, beheading. Walking, singing, beheading. The walls continued to ooze around us, and the gilded men lurched toward me leering every time they appeared, but the peculiar man's sickles sliced clean and true again and again. We filled two bags with heads. So many heads. So much violence.

"Here's the thing about it, though: I didn't feel scared or disgusted by what we were doing. I didn't feel any guilt. No, no. I felt pride. I felt alive and respected, like I was part of something very important and necessary, something beyond the usual ideas of right and wrong—some sort of balancing, maybe. I can't explain why I felt that way, but I did.

"Well, after a time, I couldn't say how long, I became tired and hungry. I'd brushed up against the maze so many times that my clothes were caked in dried blood. I told the peculiar man I needed food and a shower. He said I'd helped him a great deal but that I needed to leave for those things unless I wanted to stay in the maze forever. I didn't and said so. The man nodded and led me around a few corners and curves, to a long corridor. I saw the exit at its end. The peculiar man thanked me again and told me he'd look for me in the next maze. Then he vanished. I have no idea what he meant by that last, but I sometimes wonder if I shouldn't have left. I've never had the same sense of accomplishment out here that I did in there."

Another of our residents, Kyle Fuller, remained inside the maze for two months. Editor of our high school's newspaper and president of the school's Key Club, he entered as an idealistic and energetic kid. By the time he exited, however, he had become a specter of himself. As he later told people, "I didn't plan on being in the maze more than a day. Yeah, I had a backpack stuffed with provisions for a week, but I didn't think I'd use them. In and out with ease. That was my plan. The maze has its own plans for you, though. And its plan for me was to get caught up in a war. That sounds ridiculous, but I don't know what else to call it. It was a war.

"About an hour after going into the maze, I started to think the whole tradition was all a big joke parents played on their kids. I was like, 'This is just walking around, finding your way by the sun. No sweat.' But then everything went real dark—the middle of a deep cave kind of dark. I couldn't see my own feet, much less the maze walls. When I looked up, there were no stars. I thought maybe I'd suddenly suffered a stroke and gone blind. But then a red streak of light shot across the sky—a flare of some sort, I think—and the bright cone of a searchlight swung overhead. It lit up enough of the maze to allow me to see that I was suddenly standing in a trench surrounded by a group of people—only they weren't exactly people. They had arms and legs and unremarkable bodies, but their heads were just small, fleshy mounds dominated by enormous mouths. These beings—whatever they were—all wore uniforms that looked like army fatigues with huge, red letter Ts embroidered on the chests and each of them carried a little stick that glowed red.

"These things focused on me and began shouting to one another in a language I'd never heard. The sound of their voices tore at my ears and my eyes. I don't know if it was the pitch or the frequency or what, but I thought my head was going to explode. As they spoke, one of them pointed its glowing stick at me, and I crumpled to the ground for no apparent reason. I felt confused, more confused than I had any other time in my entire life. I couldn't remember how to stand or talk. I had to concentrate just to blink and breathe. They'd done something to my brain, made it almost shut down.

"Fear took hold of me, and I started to shiver. I couldn't stop shivering. One of the mouth-beings kicked me hard in the stomach and another kicked at my head. I couldn't understand why they were hurting me. I wanted to cry out for help but couldn't remember how to. And that's when the attack came.

"Something flew out of the darkness and shot straight through one of the mouth-beings, blowing its chest apart in a fine mist. Two more of the mouth-beings blew apart almost immediately after the first. The remainder of the beings took off running through the trench, shouting in their incomprehensible language. Their little red sticks shot beams of crimson light into the pitch-black sky. Like lasers, sort of, but with more width and intensity.

"They kept running, leaving me curled up where I lay. Above me, I heard noises like electricity sizzling through wires, like buzzsaws cutting through tin. I heard explosions all around, too, and I smelled charred meat. I got up and walked the opposite direction the mouth-things had gone, making sure to stay low. As I moved along, I found hundreds, probably thousands, of exploded bodies in the trench. Some were mouth-beings, and some were average-looking people with huge, ballooned heads, like in cheesy alien movies from the 1950s. Every so often I'd hear weird rattling footsteps or the mouth-things' screamed language, and I'd lay down among the dead and cover myself with dismembered limbs and loose organs until the sounds faded.

"I went on like this for what was apparently two months. It felt longer. A lot longer. When I ran out of water, I was forced to drink from puddles I found in the trench. Sometimes I'd throw up afterward, the water—if it was even water—burning my tongue and throat. When I ran out of food, I ignored my hunger for as long as

I could, but my legs eventually failed me and I collapsed, shaking and weak as a kitten, among the piles of the battle torn. God help me, I was out of options. I could die in a war I didn't understand, a victim of a place I didn't belong, or I could survive. I chose to survive and paid the high price survival costs. I grabbed handfuls of shredded corpse meat from around me and stuffed it in my mouth and swallowed. It didn't always stay down. Even when it did, I suffered from a constant gnawing pain in my stomach and my intestines. Was it cannibalism? I don't know. It kept me alive. I didn't want to reveal myself to the mouth-beings or the balloon heads, so I made the only choice I could.

"I kept traveling in darkness and sickness and fear. The explosions and the other weird noises never let up. Day never came. Every time I slept, I covered myself with the blanket of a mangled corpses. Sometimes I thought about giving up, lying down with the broken bodies and letting myself drift off. But I didn't. Some part of me wanted to find out where the war and the darkness ended, if they ended at all.

"I never did, though. I might have, if I'd stayed long enough, but, instead, I woke sprawled in sunlight just inside one of the maze's exits after one of my barely restful 'nights.' There was no apparent reason as to why I came back, why I was spared that dark place. I went home in a daze and received a huge celebration from my family and friends. But it didn't feel right. Nothing felt right. It still doesn't. When everything is quiet, it's almost as if I can hear distant echoes of explosions and buzzsaws and the mouth-things' blaring speech. When I blink, the darkness holds on for a millisecond longer than it used to. And food, all food, tastes a little like the putrid flesh in those trenches. Some days I wonder if I should've let myself die in that war-torn place. Some days I wonder if I actually did."

Perhaps one of the strangest stories of the maze comes from just a few years ago, courtesy of Alexis Flores, who, despite below-average grades through most of her grade school career, is now a graduate student in biochemistry on a full scholarship at a major state university, perhaps thanks to her unusual experiences during her maze journey. Alexis said of the bizarre events that, "I never expected anything odd or scary would happen in the maze. We all hear the stories and the rumors, but I don't think most of the kids believe them. I certainly didn't. For years, I'd thought the maze was the most ridiculous thing I'd ever heard of. I thought just about everything in life was ridiculous, really. So I didn't care about the maze, and I didn't bother to take much with me when I went in. Just a bottle of water and my phone. My parents complained, but that's what parents do. Taking just my phone and some water was both a mistake and a blessing, though.

"Once I was in the maze, things got spooky really fast. As soon as I turned the first corner and left the entrance out of sight, my phone started ringing. The caller ID was unknown, and the number was just a string of open and closed parentheses. I answered, because how do you not answer a call as weird as that? I wanted to know who it was. But after I said 'hello,' no one spoke. The only thing on the other end was creepy, crackly music, like from an old, beat up record player or a super old-time phonograph. It sounded out of tune—so out of tune that it stung my ears. I said 'hello' again, and the music got louder. I tried to hang up, but even after I hit the 'end call' button, the music kept playing and kept getting louder.

"The whole time I was listening to my phone, I didn't notice that my bottle of water was changing color, turning bright blue. I didn't realize it until the bottle started getting cooler. Freezing cold. Cold enough to hurt my hand. I dropped it, but even at a distance I could feel the cold growing fiercer.

"So, there I was, weird music blaring from my phone and echoing through the maze, my water bottle undergoing an icy transformation, and above it all I heard a voice speak. It had the same distorted pitch and off-kilter rhythm as the music on the phone. It said, 'Release the medium.' I looked in every direction, but I didn't see anyone attached to the voice. 'Release the medium,' it said again. I assumed it meant the water in the bottle, but I wasn't about to open that thing. You don't just accept commands from random disembodied voices, you know?

"I didn't have any idea what else to do at that point, so I took off running. Creepy music was still blasting from my phone, but at least I could leave the bottle behind. Or so I thought. When I turned the next corner, there was the bottle again, lying in the middle of the maze. I ran past it, turned another corner, and there it was again, right in front of me, glowing blue. By now, I could see my breath steaming in the air, even though it was July. Frost was forming on the walls. That's how cold the bottle was making the whole maze.

"The voice again told me to 'Release the medium.' I shouted back, 'Nope, sorry!' and landed a running kick to the bottle. It hurt my foot like hell, sort of flash froze it, but I managed to send that bottle flying. It hit a maze wall and exploded in a flash of winter. Arctic temperatures ripped through the maze. My fingers and nose and ears all went numb. I think the blood on the walls might've even gone hard.

"Out of the bottle fragments, something started moving. It was blue and glowing like the bottle had been, but it had no shape. It moved in waves, like ripples on a pond. That movement entranced me. For no reason I could explain, I wanted to dive into this thing, swim in it, maybe even drink it up. I crept up close to it, even though I was definitely getting frostbite on every bit of exposed skin and tried to figure out what it was.

"While I stared at it, I heard the voice again. It asked, 'Is this a new medium?' Maybe I should've backed away. Maybe I should've run. Instead, I reached out to the blue thing. As soon as I did, it flew at my face. I opened my mouth, half in surprise and half because, like I said, I kind of wanted to drink this thing, and the blue stuff blasted in. It didn't choke me or leak into my lungs or anything. In fact, I think it evaporated when it hit my tongue and the roof of my mouth, because when it got inside me, I inhaled a puff of the coldest, sharpest air I've ever felt. My heart skipped a couple beats and my teeth throbbed from the sudden freeze, but otherwise I was fine.

"I collected myself and ran. I reached the exit an hour or two later. I might say that what happened to me in the maze was just a bizarre hallucination or something, without any consequence, but that would be a lie. The night I left the maze, I started to think about cells and organelles and peptides and enzymes and all sorts of biology ideas that I didn't even know I'd learned. I couldn't get them out of my mind. I needed to know more. I needed to research and experiment. I needed to rearrange the building blocks of life. I'd never been so impassioned about anything before this. It was like a whole string of lights had turned on in my head.

"I guess what happened to me in the maze was good in that way. It gave me purpose, made me care. It turned me into an A student and opened new vistas of thought to me. That's all great. But there's another side. I can't tolerate heat anymore, and my resting body temperature never rises much above ninety-four degrees. I have strange, surreal dreams and waking visions of vast jellyfish-like things. It makes me wonder how much of the motivation and passion I feel is actually my own and how much was poured into me that day in the maze, by something else. Maybe it's an academic point, but I think, somehow, that answer explains everything about what happens to people in the maze. Maybe it explains even more than that."

So, what do stories such as these tell us? If we can draw any conclusions from them, which some of us argue we can't, it seems the most important is that the maze is far vaster than its strange stone facade suggests. The structure would be an oddity even without these incidents occurring within its walls, but the nature of the experiences seems to altogether imply transit to an altogether distinctly separate sphere of consciousness or reality. Something lies under the maze, something with an untapped potential for change both constructive and destructive, uplifting, and terrifying. Does this something reside in the stone walls themselves, in the unnatural blood oozing from them, in a supernatural realm beyond our ken, or within our own hearts from the very start? Who can say? All that's certain is many of us—the anxious majority, actually—can tell mind boggling stories of our unlikely travels within the maze.

Now, as I mentioned before, there *are* some teens who enter the maze and never return. We mourn these kids, lost forever in the bleeding stone. What becomes of them is wholly unknown. Some believe they live out their days in whatever instance of the maze they've fallen into, making homes for themselves, and perhaps even cultivating families and prosperity of some sort. Others believe they're all dead at the hands of unimaginable horrors, plain and simple. Occam's hungry Razor, I suppose. A few of us have proposed that these missing teens may become the blood in the walls, that the maze only expands because it keeps consuming more of its entrants. This explains the aggregate nature of the blood, at least. Whichever may be the case, we try to provide for the families of these missing teens. We bring them homemade foods and sit with them in prickly silence, but it doesn't much help. Without bodies, there is no closure. Without reasonable answers, there is no solace. We cannot hug away the mystery.

You might be thinking, "Why don't you go searching for those kids? Why don't you run into that maze in parties and pull them out?" In the past, adults tried this, or so we're told. They went in packing compasses and lights and maps and weapons—all the accoutrements of proper search and rescues. Despite their best efforts at navigation, however, the maze led them in endless circles and forced them to backtrack to its entrances when they used up their supplies. No matter how many times they subsequently resupplied and reentered and tried to solve the maze, they failed. This same fate befell so many rescue teams over the years that eventually the people of our town stopped organizing them or even discussing them as options. Now, we simply accept occasional disappearances as the way things are and continue on with our business as best we can. As I've said before, sometimes it's best to not dwell on the vagaries of the maze.

Here, you might wonder why, with the magic of technology, we don't just mount trail cameras inside the maze or fly drones over top of it to find those kids who don't return. The answer to that question is simple: recording devices don't record anything discernible when near the maze. They still run through their mechanical and technological functions, but the videos and pictures they return are grotesquely pixelated or blurred, the resulting images composed of nothing more than abstractions. In this, then, they are of no more use in returning the teens than a vivid dream or a child's fingerpainting might be.

Given the maze's predilection for swallowing up youths, the suggestion to abandon our tradition raises its head every few years. Though many of us secretly wish for such an outcome, we are fearful of what the maze may become without us and, likewise, what we may become without the maze. When the subject is raised loudly enough and frequently enough, we debate the pros and the cons of our tradition at town meetings. These meetings are, however, more like pressure release valves for the aggrieved than referendums for action because, by the end of the debates, everyone's voice has been heard and everyone's opinion has been noted, but nothing is changed. Call it apathy or disinterest or the comfort of stasis—whatever the cause, most ground swells of anger over our traditions quickly dissipate in the aftermath of the town meetings. Simply speaking of a problem seems to satisfy the majority of us.

Of course, none of this is to say that our citizens don't, rarely, shape their dissent into objects more solid than words. A tiny percentage of family members and friends of disappeared teens have attempted to destroy the maze. In days of yore, these people used pickaxes, hammers, chisels, and dynamite to try to break the maze. More modern efforts at destruction have included jackhammers, bulldozers, and industrial acids. It's from these rebels and their ferocity that we know the maze cannot be damaged, no matter the implements used to dismantle it. Pickaxes bounce off it harmlessly; explosives detonate and leave no mark. Bulldozers and jackhammers blow compressors and crack pistons long before scratching the maze's surface. For all the anger levied against it, the maze remains unbroken. We cannot destroy it. We cannot move it. We cannot prevent its growth. And thus enters the bare and basic inevitability, the fact too many of us only come to understand as weathered adults: the maze will always be with us, for better or worse. And if the maze remains, you can be certain we will send our children into its maw.

So, there you have it—the bleeding maze.

Why did I tell you about it? Why burden you with its knowledge? Well, because, if you already have a maze in your town, then it too undoubtedly grows, and if it grows, I fear the day your maze and our maze meet. What will happen then? I worry that we may be crushed. I worry that our mazes might merge and intertwine and create something far more compelling and far more dangerous than either of our individual mazes. If you have a maze, we need to plan, together, to navigate that meeting, that fused maze, and, perhaps, to eventually flee from it and leave it behind us all.

If you don't have a maze in your town, however, I believe that someday you will. I believe our maze will continue to creep beyond its borders. I believe there will come a time when there is only maze, anywhere, everywhere. When this time arrives, we will no longer be able to discern maze from not-maze nor assert with any certainty what reality "is." We will only know the experience of our journeys through the maze, with its strange fantasies and unexplained terrors. We will dimly seek for an exit, but we will find none, and we will disappear into those bleeding walls—as a people, as a species, as a world. I want you to know I believe this future awaits. I want you to understand what living with the maze means. And I want you to prepare for it as best you see fit. It's too late for our town to back away from our traditions without complete collapse, but it might not be too late for you, if you so choose. As we say to our children, "Good luck, choose your path carefully, and try not to get too bloody."

The Man in the Highchair

For many years, there lived a man in a highchair atop the roof of our city hall. We had no idea where he came from, why he took up residence on our city hall of all places, or why he spent his days and nights crammed into a piece of furniture designed for infants. We could glean no answers from him, either, because, when he first appeared, he did little more than make funny faces at those of us on the ground—the kind you might make to a baby or the kind a baby might make to you. Day and night, the man sat above our mayor's office and pruned his brow and puckered his lips and blew out his cheeks and stuck out his tongue, and we strolled by beneath him, glancing up to see what crazy facial expression we might receive when we did. Perhaps too much like babies ourselves, we chortled and pointed and thought nothing of the man except that he was a momentary amusement, an entertaining distraction, signifying nothing. Even our elected leaders, above whose offices the man had situated himself, made only the mildest of protestations against his residence, perhaps in a weak effort to curry favor with an electorate that seemed to appreciate the spectacle of the man in highchair far more than the safety of rational governance.

In those early days, if anyone did try to engage the man in the highchair in conversation, he simply responded with a string of incoherent and nonsensical syllables. "How's the weather up there today?" a passerby would shout—a favorite question of the commonfolk who thought they were being clever—and the man in the highchair would grimace and scream "Lawkerroop!" or "Magagammagaga!" or an equally meaningless jumble of sounds. We all thought it great sport to guess at the man's intent, even if we believed his words to be gibberish. The activity became so popular, in fact, that a drinking game sprouted up around the man's babble. On any given weekend night, it was common to see dozens of people standing beneath the man in the highchair, clutching paper bag-wrapped liquor bottles in their hands as they yelled out random questions and chuckled at their witty interpretations of the man's nonsense.

How the man received sustenance during his occupation of our city hall was a matter of some speculation. No one admitted to giving him food or water or, when the winter months blew in, heavy clothing and shelter, yet he never wanted for any of these resources. Indeed, as the years passed, he grew doughy and round from the sheer amount of creature comforts he somehow acquired. This corpulence led some of us to speculate that perhaps he'd hoarded food and goods in a secret locale and, even more, that he might have been climbing down from his chair during the wee hours of the night and stealing from our stores and our homes ever since he arrived.

Despite this potential criminal behavior, we didn't initially conceive of the man in the highchair as any sort of true threat. At worst, we thought of him as something akin to an embarrassing statue we had commissioned for the town but couldn't remove once it had been installed. This notion took on its greatest resonance when, one morning several summers after the man had arrived, a small glass tower unexpectedly appeared on the roof of city hall where he usually sat. Inside it perched the man, safe and comfortable on his highchair, wearing a goofy grin somehow less convivial than the ones he'd shown us in the past.

Some of us whispered that the expression was almost menacing, but in a way we couldn't exactly explain.

Who built the man's glass tower and how they'd erected it so quickly and so covertly, without anyone noticing its construction, remained a daunting mystery. Surely, we rationalized, the man hadn't fashioned it by himself. Such an endeavor was beyond a single individual, no matter how skilled with hammer and rivet that person might be. But none of us stepped forward to claim our work or offer insight into the issue. It was almost as if the man had enlisted shadow contractors from an intangible realm to build his sparkling home.

Once the man in the highchair moved into his glass house, he dragged himself and his chair outside less and less. When he did emerge, it was only once or twice per day, for twenty- or thirty-minute spans. During these public appearances, the man no longer waited for us to ask questions, but squatted above us and, without provocation, shouted his nonsense words to the world in an unbroken torrent, the tone and cadence of which began to take on a dark edge—sometimes mocking, sometimes confrontational, and sometimes shockingly violent. Though we still had no inkling of the man's true intention or message, the venom of his insensible speech seeped deep beneath our skins, inflaming the marrow of our bones. Most of us shuddered at its implications and tried to purge it from our systems; others, however, embraced it, letting it ride through their veins and curdle in the chambers of their hearts.

Those who opened themselves to the man's empty but furious rhetoric soon began to act as though they'd been possessed by a spirit of blind vengeance. They walked about town hissing epithets at anyone who didn't look like them or talk like them or mirror the righteous flames in their eyes. They insisted on guarding public restrooms with firearms so that no one but themselves could use the facilities. In stores, they elbowed smaller and physically weaker people out of checkout lines and away from prime merchandise. Heated arguments over the man in the highchair's value to our community—or lack thereof—escalated into fistfights with regularity. And all about town, lawns suddenly sprouted metal poles, atop of which flew bright red flags emblazoned with golden highchairs. Faster than we would have liked to admit, a rupture had formed beneath us, and from its depths oozed a pernicious culture of unearned rage.

If the underlying pulse of anger that beat its way through the pavement of our town had been the sole symptom of the man in the highchair's newfound—and seemingly inexplicable—influence, we could have endured the discomfort and soldiered on as a unified people. But little did we know it, anger and boorishness were to be only the first toxins to leach into our lives.

Not long after the rippling red flags began to occlude our stars, the man's glass tower underwent expansions—major expansions. First, it gained a more substantial foundation, which, when completed, filled the entirety of our town hall's roof surface. Then, it sprouted two wings that draped over the sides of the hall and hung halfway to the ground like enormous, cubist icicles. Finally, it rose higher—roughly three times its original height, making it by far the tallest structure in our town.

Just as before, the parties responsible for the construction went unknown, with building taking place in the depths of night and proceeding with uncanny speed. We'd tuck in for a full evening's rest and wake to new, utterly completed extensions of the tower's reach. No screech of steel against steel ever split our sleep. No bright light that might indicate work ever emanated from within the tower's vicinity. No convoy of construction vehicles ever rumbled by our homes like a herd of stampeding bulls. The man's tower simply expanded, as though feeding off the fury of his adherents.

A few enterprising and inquisitive souls among us became so unnerved by this invisible workforce that they set up streaming video cameras in trees and bushes and streetlights adjacent to city hall in an effort to try to capture the builders in action. The results of their sleuthing, however, did little to dispel the mystery or pacify any of our anxieties. Most nights the cameras caught nothing; the tower stood rigid and imposing, but without any hint of growth. Other nights, at random points in time, an unusually undersized hand on an otherwise adult arm reached out from the darkness at the right edge of the video feed and grasped toward the cameras' lenses. An abrupt cut to what appeared to be a pile of writhing, half-charred human bodies followed the grabbing motion. The stream then dropped and couldn't be reestablished. Every morning that followed one of these particular nights, we woke to discover that the tower had added new dimensions and new features. After three weeks of witnessing the same pattern of mind-numbing stasis and nocturnal horror show without any explanation to show for their efforts, the amateur detectives packed up their gear and backed away, defeated by the illogic of the entire experience. We were more concerned about the tower's rapid ascent than ever before, but, armed with the knowledge that it held to no laws or reason that we understood, we had no idea what actions to take or how to proceed in order to prevent it from clawing higher.

As the glass palace continued to encroach further into our world, the man in the highchair's supporters became bolder and more brazen. Every day, by the hundreds, they organized beneath the tower, setting up lawn chairs and picnic blankets and outdoor grills as if at a music festival or a tailgating event. They painted the man's nonsense words on huge posterboard signs and, snarling like rabid dogs and feral cats, held them aloft like oblations to a god. From an invisible vendor, they purchased miniature red flags adorned by highchairs, and these they waved furiously or pinned to their clothes. If an unfortunate wandered into the gathering without a flag, that person was forcibly removed from the city hall grounds, often with much shoving and literal arm twisting, if not a small amount of bloodletting.

When the man in the highchair finally made his appearances above the massed, flag-bearing throngs, they ceased all motion and listened to his inarticulate ravings with rapt attention. If at any point he paused during his "addresses," they took up his mantle, imitating to the last guttural inflection whatever verbal sludge he had just vomited upon them. In this way, the gatherings might have best been described as call and response religious services or Greek stage tragedies in which the chorus had nothing of consequence to say for itself.

Beyond the tower, the man's supporters began to exhibit far more distressing behavior. They walked about town parroting the man's bitter nonsense words and dropping them into conversation whenever possible. The same words sometimes functioned as verbs, sometimes nouns, and sometimes adjectives or adverbs—it seemed that their use was predicated on arbitrary factors, if it was predicated on anything at all. We questioned the supporters about their speech and tried explaining to them that it conveyed no ideas beyond unchained anger, but this tactic invariably resulted in assault. No sooner would we level a criticism than the supporters would dissolve into blind rage, flailing out with their fists in an effort to dislodge teeth and break noses, to fill our mouths with so much blood that we could no longer dissect their utterances.

We reported these incidents to our local police, but they hid behind a thin blue smirk. They assured us our cases would be investigated. They told us that our lives would be protected at all costs. They even went as far as to haul a supporter or two off to their station for purported booking. But as soon as we turned our backs to them, they snickered and winked and murmured amongst themselves unmistakable fragments of the man in the highchair's vicious garble.

With little other civil recourse left to us, we petitioned our mayor and city council members to remove the man in the highchair and his tower from city hall or, at very least, impose strict penalties on his supporters' increasing violence. To these requests, however, we received nothing more than mannequin stares and blank letters of response. It was as though the pulp of our elected officials had been completely cored away, leaving behind human rinds incapable of simple action, let alone serious aid.

All the while, the crowds beneath the man in the highchair grew thicker, more raucous. They burned effigies of faceless women, of papier-mâché dolls painted black and brown. They brought firearms to their gatherings and discharged them into the clouds in a war with reason itself. And when the man lumbered from his tower and spoke to them, they cheered and cried and pumped their fists in triumph. He held them mesmerized with his anti-rhetoric, his void tongue. He spouted his usual vitriolic nonsense words and the supporters below nodded in approval, clapping and roaring at random intervals as though they understood the man's intent. This led us to wonder: Did the man beckon his followers to him with a whistle only certain ears are attuned to? Was he speaking a language we couldn't hear? Or were his words merely a mirror for a formless malice that always already stirred within his supporters' chests? It was impossible to determine the truth.

As the crowds grew, so, too, did the tower stretch its vast wings. They spread high over our small city, in all directions. They hung above our business district, our hospital, our schools, and our county jail. City hall itself became totally encased in glass, its entrances and exits blocked by dozens of thick panes. We witnessed this same excessive layering everywhere across the tower—now more a castle or fortress, in truth. The structure seemed to be growing on its own, hiding itself away beneath an infinite series of surfaces, making of itself a matryoshka complex. And inside, at the core of his bellicose universe, roiled the man in the highchair.

Between gatherings, we glimpsed him lumbering along many random corridors, screaming, and snarling at invisible enemies, his jowls a quivering mass of ochre jelly. He moved about his tower without apparent aim, content to be led by momentary whim and desire. His highchair, which, at this point, had been gilded and encrusted with gems by unknown parties, stood sentry at the entryway to his sanctum. Even though his newfound power over nearly half our populace seemed to invigorate him and send him wandering through his glass labyrinth more frequently, it was in the chair that he still slept and ate and defecated.

With the man in the highchair's influence casting an ever-darkening shadow over our lives, we found ourselves at a crossroads. We knew we couldn't allow the man and his fanatics free reign over our town, yet we possessed no readily tangible means of resistance. Our peacekeepers had become corrupt, our politics had been rendered impotent, and our law was dissolving further with every acrid bawl that dribbled from the man's puckered mouth. We were, ourselves, the last line of defense against the insanity of the highchair. Knowing this, some of our numbers chose to organize and march against the man's supporters when they gathered. Armed with homemade signs and rhyming chants, these bold protestors went to meet the worshippers of the highchair and attempt a vocal opposition to the wrath that had ensnared our home. They left excited, energized, ready to throw their bodies forward as the sword of justice. They held their heads high and laughed—nervously, at times—about the surprise they'd give the man's supporters. We truly believed this was a step in the right direction, a step that mattered. We truly believed we'd reached a turning point.

As it turned out, we would never see or hear from any of those protestors again. We waited for them to return, to give us an update on the opposition effort, but they never did. When we went looking for them, we turned up nothing. At city hall, the supporters milled about as usual; at police central booking, the on-duty officers dismissed us, saying no arrests had been made; at individual protestors' homes, cars sat unmolested, and doors and windows remained locked tight. An unsettling shroud of normalcy hung over the disappearances. We prayed that mass vanishings weren't part of the new usual, but the usual, we were quickly learning, signified little more than the particular insanities we were willing to accept on any given day.

Soon after the protestors went missing, we sought outside aid, calling the state police and the FBI, not to mention friends and family members who lived outside our city limits. However, our calls could not be placed, and the line dropped to hungry, waiting silence whenever we rang outside parties. If we pressed the issue and continued calling, our phones returned thousands of strings of meaningless text message, then overheated and died. Social media apps and pages through which we could have made pleas for help mysteriously loaded blank, bereft of the option to post updates or message contacts.

With digital avenues rendered impassible, we took to our cars, our bikes, our feet. We tried to leave the man and his insane supplicants behind. But, as we found out, we couldn't. At the edges of our city there now sliced a colossal white wall that loomed over our tallest buildings and our oldest trees. The wall cut through highway and sidewalk, forest, and stream. Where it stood, soil and stone had been violently rent, as though it had burst from a fault line in the earth. Its milky smooth surface glistened as though wet, reminding us of false teeth and glass eyes. When we reached out to touch it in hopes of scaling its heights, our fingers swelled painfully, and our chests tightened. Breath came in short, rapid bursts and our vision blurred. We couldn't fathom how a structure—even one as bizarre as the wall before us—could affect us in the same way as an allergen or a venom, yet that was precisely the case.

Lacking resources to safely mount the wall and concerned about our health, we fled back to our homes. We needed to plan more diligently, to organize more comprehensively. We needed strategy beyond knee-jerk fear. So we met late at night, in our garages, in our basements, and we carved out paths to resistance, if not escape. We planned days of unified strike, sit-ins at government buildings beside city hall, and marches through our streets. The steam of revolution began to waft from our windows. But as we planned and prepared, as we made ready to collapse the order of aggression that had taken over our city, people from our ranks began to disappear.

Just as the protestors had, our non-supporter friends, neighbors, and colleagues vanished without sight or sound of struggle, without a goodbye or a message of despondent surrender. Rumors of tan military-style trucks prowling our neighborhoods under moonlight circulated through our numbers. More than a few of us saw a trio of blue-suited men with identical, red-mottled faces staring at the homes of the vanished from nearby sidewalks or lawns. We even witnessed computer and television screens flashing momentary, almost subliminal, images of wild, puffy eyes and mass graves. When we added these incidents to the disappearances and weighted the value of their import, the math of implication resulted in a frightening sum.

Even knowing that we might be snuffed into twirling wisps of memory at any given time, we tried to continue living as best we could. We watched television and browsed the Internet, but all stations and all websites had been reduced to a single live-streamed video of the main entrance to the man's tower. We slumped off to work and ran necessary errands, but when we ventured beyond our front doors, we inevitably encountered the man's supporters who, by this time, used his incoherent speech as their primary lexicon and spat hulking wads of phlegm in our faces when we failed to understand their anti-language. Any further perceived slight we made against these people brought down upon us a flurry of fists and boot heels. Those of us who defended ourselves with reciprocal force ended up being dragged away by law enforcement and, in all cases, erased from the world. As a last resort, we tried to take refuge in the asylum of literature, but every book in the city—indeed, even those in our own collections—had been, impossibly, scrubbed clean of words. Only a grim narrative of periods and question marks remained between their covers.

While we dealt with the travails of daily life under the man in the highchair's dominion, his tower spread out across our sky like a vast crystalline mushroom cloud, blocking the firmament with a multifaceted glass ceiling. We could barely see the sun, the moon, or the stars without the lens of the man's tower distorting our view. We could barely see anything but the tower, hanging over us every hour of every day. And still our ranks were sucked into oblivion by cloned men in blue suits. And still the man in the highchair vented noxious sentiment into the atmosphere and our vital institutions. And still the man's supporters rallied to his tower and pledged allegiance to his maniacal bluster.

Now here we are, glass wholly encasing our world, the man in the highchair a step removed from godhood, and ourselves shades of the people we once thought we were. We know what we must do if we are to survive—the only course of action left to us. We must pick up the heaviest rocks we can carry, the most solid bricks we can find, and we must throw them, hard and fast and far and true. We must launch them from slings and catapults and homemade cannons. We must not be afraid of the sound of shattering glass or cracking bone. We must not worry about the grievous wounds we are sure to sustain. The man in the highchair and his adherents have chosen to destroy us, to remake our city as Pandaemonium. They cast the first stone, the second stone, every stone. Now let us cast our own. Let the man in the highchair be sliced to ribbons when his grand palace splinters above his head. Let his followers take cover and hide as we've had to hide or let them face the same mincing hail. Let us dance in the shower of glass and know we are free. This is our plan. This is our hope. We must succeed so that our city serves not as a forgotten tragedy or a cautionary tale, but as a legend of resistance for ages to come.

The Richview Massacre

People consume pizza the world over. Its simplicity lends itself to ubiquity. This is especially true in the United States, where even the smallest towns in parts of the nation virtually devoid of Italian influence have at least one pizza parlor. Like football and SUVs and readily available firearms, pizza is part of the American character. Indeed, with over three billion pies sold in the country every year, the Statue of Liberty should probably hold aloft a slice of pepperoni with extra cheese rather than a torch of enlightenment.

Yet, despite the deep ingratiation of pizza in American life, there exists a tiny rural town in the heartland of the nation where not a single person will feast on its greasy deliciousness—at least, not anymore. This town? Richview, Ohio. And the reason no one in Richview will touch pizza? Well, that's a complicated matter.

One could be facile and say the denizens of Richview are all paranoid fearmongers trapped in the past. But such an answer doesn't reckon with the town's admittedly disturbing history. See, years ago, Richview fell victim to a massacre, but not of any conventional—or even explainable—sort. This massacre involved no assault rifles or school buildings, no bombs or terrorists. It possessed no message or motive or even the steadying presence of clear perpetrators. No, the people of Richview faced a massacre unlike any other in the annals of crime or warfare. Theirs was a massacre wrapped in the folds of the unknown, a massacre dipped in rumor and mystery, a massacre that could only be understood somehow, someway, as a result of pizza.

Statement of Michael Johns, Owner of Old Country Tool & Farm Supply

"The night it happened, I closed up the store at seven and stayed after to do some stock work. Well, when I do my stocking, I take a lot of breaks where I kinda zone out and stare out the front doors of the store. That night was the same. I was stocking and staring, stocking, and staring. Slice Masters was right across the road, so it was what I usually stared at. I liked to watch people come and go, see who I knew that was going for pizza. Always interesting. People went into the place with a thin, wanting look and they came out all smiles and flushed faces. Me, I could never eat there. Lactose intolerant for years. But I heard Slice Masters was damn fine pizza. Always heard that. Best pizza for three counties, so they said.

"Anyways, yeah, I was staring right at the place when the massacre must've been happening. I didn't see anyone go in who seemed peculiar. Just people from around town. You know, people who should've been there. No one carrying a weapon or anything. No one looking like they wanted to kick someone's teeth in. Nope. Didn't hear anything either. No broken windows. No screaming or hollering. Didn't see anything through their windows except motion. I assumed it was just people moving around. In fact, if you told me that more than a dozen people was getting killed inside that place that night, while I was watching it, I would've laughed at you. It wasn't different from any other night.

"Well, except for one thing, maybe. Only one thing. At the time, I thought it was my old, tired eyes, but now, now I have to consider that maybe it wasn't. See, at one point while I was stocking, not too long after I saw the Dandelion girl go in, I thought I saw a thing flash away from Slice Masters, real fast. A white-colored thing. Not very tall, but long. Real long. As long as two cars. It seemed to melt out of the wall of the building. Then it stretched out and shot away, like a rubber band. Was it anything? I don't know. Maybe just shadows and car lights playing tricks. But I guess it could've been something else. I guess it could've."

13 Facts about the Massacre, Part 1

Fact 1: On the evening of December 11, 2004, at approximately 7:20pm, seventeen-year-old Jessica Dandelion, a junior at Richview High School, entered Richview's sole pizzeria, Slice Masters, to pick up an order of four extra-large pizzas—all plain cheese—for a secret holiday party she was throwing while her parents were out of town. However, Ms. Dandelion never received her pizzas, and she never made it to her party because, as she walked into Slice Masters, she discovered seventeen dead bodies sprawled out within the restaurant. She later described the scene to reporters as "horrible and unreal, like one of those old black and white films about war they show us in history class. The ones with, like, people who were shot or gassed or whatever just lying all over the place. It was the same, but with people I knew."

Fact 2: According to medical examiners' reports, the cause of death for all the individuals in Slice Masters was either strangulation or suffocation, and their times of death were within minutes of one another, if not simultaneous. Given that Ms. Dandelion placed her phone order at approximately 7:00pm that same evening and nothing about the Slice Masters' employee's tone over the phone seemed unusual to her, we can assume the deaths occurred within the brief twenty-minute window after Ms. Dandelion's call but before her arrival at the pizzeria.

Fact 3: First responders initially suspected a leaking gas line had inundated the pizzeria with odorless toxic fumes and caused the deaths. However, Ms. Dandelion reported no lightheadedness or nausea upon entering the restaurant, which she almost certainly would have if the space had been filled with carbon monoxide. The theory also lacked any reasonable explanation for the existence of strangulation victims, whose necks clearly evidenced signs of violent constriction, as though from a length of rope. A utilities inspection conducted at Slice Masters after the massacre found no leaks in the building's gas line, either, ultimately ruling out the possibility of such an explanation.

Statement of Jessica Dandelion, Initial Witness
"It was about seven when I called for the pizza. Krista and me, that's Krista Fuller, my best friend, we were trying to throw a party. My mom and dad didn't know. They're at my aunt's place in Cincinnati for the weekend. She's really sick. Cancer. Brain cancer. It's sad. But, yeah, we were having a party and we needed food, so I called Slice Masters cause they have great pizza. Pizza's easy, you know? Everyone'll eat it and it can sit out forever. We needed something like that cause we invited a lot of people from school. Krista bought six cases of beer, and the guy she's dating was gonna bring some weed... um... I probably shouldn't say any more about that, but, yeah, it was supposed to be a pretty kick-ass party, so we needed good food.

"When I called Slice Masters, the dude who answered didn't sound nervous or scared or anything. Nah. He just sounded like a guy answering a phone at a pizza place. Maybe a little, um, hurried. Or busy. But that was it.

"I left Krista at my place around seven-ten, and I got to Slice Masters around seven-twenty. There were about eight cars in the parking lot, which is pretty normal for a weekend night. Like I said, Slice Masters has great pizza.

"So, I park and go in and the first thing that hits me is like, a bread smell. Or yeast, I guess. My mom bakes sometimes. Whatever it was, it was really strong. And under that was another smell. Like in an old porta-potty. Piss. Shit. We learned in bio that's what happens to people when they die. They just... they can't hold it in.

"Anyway, I'm smelling this weird mix of smells, and I know something's not right. I can smell it, yeah, but I can feel it too. It's like, you know when you walk in a room where people have just been fighting or were about to have sex, and you interrupt accidentally? There's a... a vibration to the room. A quiet vibration. That's how it was in the pizza place. Like I walked in on something intense that had just stopped.

"I go further into the place, and I see the people. I knew they were dead. Their faces were all a bruised shade of purple. Nobody's that color unless something awful's happened to them. Some of their eyes were bugged out, too. And some of their tongues were dangling out of their mouths, the same purple color as their faces.

"I started shaking, and I almost vomited. I think I was screaming 'Oh my God,' but I'm not sure. It's strange. I remember screaming, I remember the fear, but I don't remember the words I screamed. I think I called out for help, too, but of course no one answered.

"At some point, I picked up the phone next to the cash register and dialed 9-1-1. It took the operator like ten minutes to understand what I meant when I said, 'Everyone in Slice Masters is dead.' He thought it was a threat or something. But eventually he sent help.

"While I waited for the police and the ambulances to come, I didn't hear any doors or windows close. I didn't hear anybody leave or enter. Everything was so quiet, except for a loud sucking noise in the walls or maybe in the pipes, but that didn't last long. No idea what that sound was. I didn't check. I just froze where I stood and stared at one of the dead people: Bill Spoke.

"I knew Mr. Spoke for years. He was a single dad. Ex-wife has a meth problem, so she isn't really around. His son, Danny, is in my class. We hang out sometimes. As I stared at Mr. Spoke's swelled-up face, I kept thinking, Danny's never going to see his dad again. He's not gonna be in the audience for Danny's graduation. He's not gonna see Danny get married or open the woodworking store Danny talks about. And all I could feel was sadness, not for the unfairness or because it made me think of my own dad or anything like that, but because Mr. Spoke died for apparently no other reason than that he wanted pizza on the wrong night. What a crazy thing to die for, right? Pizza."

13 Facts about the Massacre, Part 2

Fact 4: In lieu of gas inhalation, police and forensic investigators turned their attention toward toxic agents to which the victims may have been exposed. Intentional poisoning by staff or unintentional ingestion of certain toxic fungi or mold could have provided explanation for the mass asphyxiation. Toxicology reports, though, revealed no trace of harmful substances within Slice Masters or the victims' bodies. Ingestion of toxins also did not account for the strangulation deaths. Thus, this potential solution was discarded as well.

Fact 5: Although medical examiners observed no poisons or toxins in the blood or organs of Slice Masters victims, they *did* note an inexplicable consistency: the swollen esophagus of each and every suffocation victim contained unswallowed traces of raw pizza dough.

Fact 6: Outside the victims, police found the Slice Masters premises utterly devoid of dough—a most unusual state for a popular pizzeria during prime business hours. The business's counters were barren, its ovens gaped open and empty, and even its freezer, which was ajar when investigators arrived, held no premade dough.

Statement of Sarah Stetzel, Wife of Slice Masters Owner John Stetzel
"John opened the place in ninety-two. It had been his dream to own a restaurant. He lived to cook. I was always surprised he chose pizza, but he said that it would sell well in Richview. I couldn't argue. And, for a country boy who couldn't even point out Sicily on a map, he *did* make a good pizza.

"Sometimes I think Slice Masters was John's real baby. See, we couldn't have children because of a medical issue with John's urethra. We didn't have the money for IVF or adoption, either. So I think the pizzeria became his child, in a sense. He spent so much time there, even after business took off. For years, he worked twelve- or fourteen-hour days slapping dough and pouring sauce. Last year I finally got him to cut back. Eight hours max or else. Still, he filled in whenever anyone wanted a day off or called in sick. He wouldn't neglect his baby. And that's what happened the night of the... incident. John filled in on when he wasn't even supposed to be there.

"The morning of the day John died, one of his chefs—an older man named Paul Cody—came down with the flu, and

John told him to stay home, that John would go in and cook the entire afternoon and evening. John was supposed to be off work. He'd been at the shop the past eight straight days, and we were supposed to drive into Columbus and go Christmas shopping. But, like I said, that's how John was, loyal to his employees and his restaurant. I think the employees loved him for it, at least. They threw him a birthday party every year. I mean, who does that for their boss? That's why I can't imagine anyone would do... well... the thing that happened.

"Everyone else in Richview loved John's place, too. Never a bad word around town. John said it was entirely because of the pizza. It was a... what did he call it... a social currency. Above all else, he prided himself on the crust. Said the crust was the foundation for the entire business. He went out of his way to buy crazy expensive designer flour and yeast for the shop. I didn't ask too much about it. No one else did, either. As long as the pizza tasted great, everybody just nodded and tuned John out when he geeked out over his flours and his yeasts. Just recently he'd gotten in the mail a weird metal box with a vacuum-sealed vial of some kind of yeast culture in it. He said it was extremely rare and no other pizzerias had it, that he'd ordered it from a guy on a message board on the Internet. He said it would cause the pizza to taste 'out of this world.' I thought the entire thing was a little ridiculous, but, you know, it was his passion.

"He took that yeast with him the night *it* happened. He told me he might try it that evening and that he'd bring a couple test slices back for me if it really was as good as advertised. I said I just wanted him to be home as soon as he could. I thought maybe we'd go look for presents the next day. But there was no next day, not for any of us.

"You know, I hope John was happy that night before it happened. I hope he got to taste a slice made from his new yeast at least once before... well... the end. I hope that taste, whatever it was, made him smile. Sometimes I wonder if he thought he could make a perfect pizza and it would be his child, his legacy. Sometimes I wonder if he loved that restaurant more than me. I guess I'll never know."

13 Facts about the Massacre, Part 3

Fact 7: Signs of struggle littered the pizzeria. In the dining area, most of the tables had been flipped on their sides, spilling plates and cups and condiments of all variety. Several patrons had lost glasses and shoes in a scuffle. In the kitchen, a field of knives and forks lay scattered on the floor, and the three on-duty staff members clutched cleavers and butcher knives in their hands, as though for defense. Whatever happened in Slice Masters had been, without question, a violent affair.

Fact 8: A half hour after local law enforcement's arrival at the scene, a fleet of white vans surrounded Slice Masters and cordoned off all the land in an approximately one-mile radius from the pizzeria. People in hazmat uniforms rolled out razor wire barricades and remained posted at the breaks along the barricades' lengths, brandishing assault rifles. Gray-suited officials from an unknown agency instructed homeowners within the quarantine zone to remain inside their houses until investigation teams completed what these officials claimed was "an ongoing sweep of the area." This "sweep" lasted a full forty-eight hours, after which time the barriers were rolled up and the white vans departed, never to be seen in Richview again.

Fact 9: Major media outlets barely covered the massacre. Although the circumstances surrounding the deaths were ripe for speculation and sensationalism, only a fringe handful of newspapers and Internet sites published reports about the incident. Those that did so received anonymous threatening phone calls ordering the articles be pulled and most had their servers hacked and databases wiped of all stories and research related to Richview. Thus, within a year of the incident, shoddy conspiracy websites and obscure discussion boards had become the sole sources of information on the subject.

Statement of Lincoln Fuller, Crime Reporter for the Columbus Herald-Dispatch

"You've got a coverup in Richview, plain and simple. But a coverup of what, I don't exactly understand.

"I went out to Richview the day after the massacre on a tip from a police contact and tried to talk to the now-infamous gray suits from the white vans. You know, get a little insider info. But every last one of those expressionless creeps wouldn't say more to me than 'We have the situation under control' and 'We're investigating the causes of the deaths.' They wouldn't tell me who they worked for, they wouldn't tell me why they'd set up a quarantine, and they wouldn't discuss the facts of the crime. When I tried to pry on any issue, they waved their rifles at me and told me to move on. 'We have shoot-to-kill authorization,' they said. 'And we will use it if necessary.'

"I've butted heads with some tough cops over the years, but these gray suits were different. They didn't threaten me out of malice or some dominance bullshit; they threatened me because they truly believed maintaining the perimeter was a life-or-death matter. That scared me. And, obviously, stoked my curiosity.

"I interviewed some bystanders and some of the first responders and then took off for home. I spent the next week researching everything I could about Richview and Slice Masters and John Stetzel and the victims whose names the local PD released. Mostly, I found nothing. Richview had never produced any historical relevance other than the massacre. Slice Masters had no ties to organized crime or questionable business practices. And the victims' biographies read like Hallmark greeting cards. I dug up no leads. It frustrated me. Drove me crazy. Despite what most people think, violence rarely occurs in a vacuum. Yet in Richview, in this bastion of unremarkable plainness, violence had exploded with an unthinkable force.

"As I was hitting dead ends again and again, one comment Susan Stetzel made during my interview with her kept picking at me. She said John had ordered a weird silver box of what she thought was yeast. I couldn't stop wondering if what was inside that box wasn't yeast. What if John Stetzel had inadvertently gotten mixed up in the drug trade? Plenty of rural communities like Richview play home to meth dealers and opiate peddlers. If John had pissed off the wrong people, he may have faced dire repercussions.

"So I tried to track the package Susan mentioned. Its return address was listed as a post office box in Dulce, New Mexico. When I called the post office in Dulce, the workers there said the name of the box holder had been scrubbed from their computer systems without their knowledge and that no paper records existed. Shut down again, I jumped on the message board John had ordered the box from—a normal baking forum as far as I could tell—and hunted for the user he'd been in contact with about the special yeast. 'Rendlesham,' as this user called themselves on the board, had touted an 'incredibly rare, specially engineered yeast with almost instant rise time and a universe of flavor you've never tasted' in multiple threads. John Stetzel had been the only individual to engage in serious conversation about purchasing the stuff.

"My next move was obvious: I tried to find an identity or contact info for 'Rendlesham.' No luck. The user hadn't filled out any personal info in the message board's profile, and a trace of Rendlesham's IP address led to an organization called Archuleta Mesa RF, which I couldn't find any Internet presence or contact info for. No such business or non-profit seemed to exist.

"Through my scouring of leads, I *did* discover something, though: namely, that Dulce is popular in UFO circles as part of a wild legend. A bunch of people who study UFOs believe that the government runs some sort of ultra-secret extraterrestrial biological research base there. It's supposedly close to Dulce, under a place called—drum roll, please—Archuleta Mesa. The registered name for the IP address. Archuleta Mesa RF. Archuleta Mesa Research Facility.

"According to UFO researchers, alien organisms both living and dead are kept at the Dulce research facility and are the frequent subjects of government experiments. Some ufologists claim that scientists there have engineered new bioweapons based on alien biology. Others claim the facility's researchers have created hybrid terrestrial-extraterrestrial organisms. And a few even claim that, every so often, one of those weapons or hybrids gets out.

"Now, what does that bit of crazy trivia mean for Richview? Like I said, I don't know. I searched for a long time but couldn't figure it out. I flew to UFO conventions and talked to people who are convinced we're ruled by reptile creatures from other worlds. I arranged meetings with government employees from the Pentagon, the Department of Homeland Security, and the Center for Disease Control. No one told me anything of worth. So I stopped. I had to let it go. I had to face the fact that either someone's using the urban legend of the Dulce facility as a successful screen for murder or there's something substantial and very much conspiratorial about the facility's legend. One way or the other, John Stetzel definitely ordered a whole lot more than he bargained for when he bought that yeast."

13 Facts about the Massacre, Part 4

Fact 10: A month after the massacre, the abandoned Slice Masters building burned to the ground in what local fire crews called "the hottest blaze anyone's ever seen here, like the tongues of hell." The fire raged so hot that the entirety of the pavement in the parking lot melted and oozed onto an adjacent roadway. Firefighters suspected arson because of the intense heat, but Richview Fire and Rescue possessed no funds to open an investigation and Ohio state authorities expressed outright hostility toward the notion of arson, so the origins of the blaze were never probed.

Fact 11: Following the destruction of Slice Masters, residents of Richview began smelling the overpowering scent of bread at random locations around town. Backyard gardens, attics, church basements, minivans, the elementary school gymnasium, and the restrooms at an old gas station in town: the odor seeped into all these and many other places. Soon, everyone in Richview had experienced it at least once, if not many times. The odor was, as some Richview citizens said, "not a pleasant, warm bread smell like you're used to, but strange and unsettling, almost like the cold chemical smell in a hospital room." Others drew ghostly allusions, saying that the scent "wanders the land haunting us so that we won't forget what happened in the Slice Masters." Though the odor persists to this day and is still smelled at various times and in various locations in the Richview area, no one has yet uncovered its source. The manifestation of the smell also coincided with a precipitous drop in bread and pasta consumption in Richview and is, in all likelihood, one of the catalysts for the town's unspoken prohibition on pizza.

Fact 12: Richview is primarily a farming community, with tens of thousands of acres of land dedicated to the cultivation of soybeans and sheep. At the same time that the "unsettling" bread scent drifted into Richview, the town and its outlying areas began to experience devastating livestock deaths. Farmers reported dozens of sheep killed by unknown means, often with no outward sign of violence. In the few cases where veterinarians examined the carcasses, they discovered a proliferation of unidentifiable fungal spores in the animals' airways and lungs. Tests also revealed that, bizarrely, none of the sheep possessed any glucose in their blood—a dangerous condition that was blamed for their demise. How dozens of sheep could suddenly become hypoglycemic no one could explain. Like the odor, this mystery also abides to the present, as domesticated animals in and near Richview are still occasionally found dead and drained of their vital sugars.

Statement of Katherine Reich, former Mayor of Richview, Ohio
"After the Slice Masters massacre, Richview collapsed upon itself. Everyone in Richview knew someone who had been killed. We're a very small town, after all. A pallor hung over everything we did. No one wanted to work. No one wanted to eat. Definitely, no one wanted to celebrate the holidays. Really, the only activity people threw themselves into was conjecture about what had happened at Slice Masters. Every day people came to my office with so many off-the-wall theories that I could've written them down and sold a book. Mafia dons and drugged-up teens and escaped serial killers and aliens and government experiments gone wrong: I heard it all. And I understood. We wanted

answers, even if the answers were absurd. Answers would've given us closure. But there simply weren't—and still aren't—any answers.

"Eventually, we fell back into our routines. We farmed. We watched television. We talked about Ohio State football and the president over beers. The usual topics. The safe topics. If a dozen sheep died on someone's farm, we didn't discuss it. We knew the deaths were connected to Slice Masters, somehow. We saw our lost friends and loved ones in every one of those dead sheep. But we didn't talk about it. If we had, it would've further salted a wound that just won't heal.

"Now, years after the massacre, we go about our days pretty much like we did before it, but with little changes. If we're outside at night, we carry brighter flashlights and glance over our shoulders more than most people. If we go to a restaurant, we enter a little slower, a little more carefully, than anyone not from around here might. When we cook, we lock our doors and our windows. And, of course, we don't eat pizza.

"I can't blame anyone around here for not eating pizza, honestly. We can't stomach the stuff anymore. Too many bad associations. And the smell. It's too much like the damned mystery odor that comes from nowhere. That's real, by the way. I've experienced it several times. Every time I catch a whiff, my hands start shaking and I wonder if it's my time to be one of the people in Slice Masters. I imagine how those people must have felt. And it tears me apart. So, no, I don't think it's unreasonable that we avoid pizza. How can we eat it when it reminds us of all the senseless horror in the world? How can we do that to ourselves?"

13 Facts about the Massacre, Part 5

Fact 13: Occasionally, the farmers of Richview find cinder block sized chunks of what seems to be hardened dough in their fields.

Occasionally, hunters in Richview encounter thickets of trees that have been slicked by some sort of wet, unrecognizable fungus. Occasionally, Richview children stumble upon rustling bushes infused with the odor of breadstuffs. And occasionally paramedics from Richview respond to calls where they discover a person dead in their home or their yard or their car, a victim of asphyxiation without apparent cause. These deaths, these occasional deaths, are always ruled suicides and no one in Richview chooses to argue with that conclusion. They're too busy eating at the new burger place in town, anyway. Everyone loves it. Owned by a corporate conglomerate based hundreds of miles away, it's remarkably conventional. Its slogan: "Burgers and fries, grilled simply and simply grilled." It doesn't smell like anything other than grilled meat, and no one's died in its confines. People in Richview say it's the best restaurant the town's ever had.

Extinction in Green

Day 1: We cannot leave this windowless basement room, for the emerald light outside has become too fierce and the noises we hear within it have become all too unfamiliar.

Day 2: We do not know the source of the light, only that it began yesterday morning when it washed over us in place of dawn and, brighter than the glint in a god's eye, blotted out the world.

Day 3: Our dying phones find no reception, so our messages of panic and confusion go unsent and unread.

Day 4: Water continues to flow from the pipes, and electricity continues to twist through the basement wires, but for how long and to what end?

Day 5: Muffled chitterings and moans from beyond the ceiling filter down to us and make us dream of anthills high as skyscrapers and infirmaries staffed by roach physicians—images from a world we no longer understand.

Day 6: The basement is divided into three sections: a storage area stocked with canned goods and bottled water, a laundry room we've converted to a bathroom, and a rec room replete with couch, billiard table, and minibar.

Day 7: There are five of us, all strangely nondescript beyond our skin tones and our performed genders, all without significant external markers that might lead to deeper characterizations.

Day 8: We refuse to reveal our names to one another, as naming ourselves would provide too much reality to a situation we pray might yet be nothing more than an exceptionally vivid nightmare.

Day 9: We spend too much time inside our heads, constructing meaning for the incessant scratching on the walls above us and envisioning the innumerable ways we will all suffer before we can finally rest.

Day 10: We are lucky that the basement is well stocked with beans and dried fruits and all manner of nonperishable foodstuffs, otherwise who knows what measures we may have had to take.

Day 11: Our cycle of night and day has been replaced by a cycle of general exhaustion and complete collapse.

Day 12: Silence rules our waking hours, as there is little to speak of other than our fears, and the proper words do not exist to give them voice.

Day 13: This afternoon we noticed that a strip of searing viridescence now outlines the basement door, a fact which leads us to believe the light has grown even stronger, even brighter since we took refuge here.

Day 14: Are our families and our friends still alive somewhere and, if so, are they still human?

Day 15: Today we heard footfalls above, followed by a single, hollow scream that quickly faded to a rubbery squeal, as if from a punctured balloon in its final exhalations.

Day 16: Many of us murmur the names of our loved ones in our sleep and grasp at empty spaces where warm, knowing bodies once nestled against us.

Day 17: If five random passersby become trapped in the home of a stranger for the rest of their lives, does it make them a family?

Day 18: We debated the virtues of unlocking and opening the door to the basement for a momentary peek outside our safe haven but decided that the reward of knowing would not have outweighed the consequence of seeing.

Day 19: I must force myself to keep these records short, given that there is only one small notepad in the basement, and I intend for it to last as long as we do.

Day 20: A pungent odor as of burning wires entered the basement this morning, accompanied by a chorus of feverish clicks and disjointed groans from above; hours later, neither has dissipated.

Day 21: We wonder what project is being undertaken in the world beyond this basement: war, assimilation, extermination, or an enterprise so alien that we cannot begin to even grasp its edges?

Day 22: All the canned food we eat tastes of salt and rusted metal—the flavor of survival, of desperation, of unremitting imprisonment.

Day 23: A brief flash of darkness broke through the green light today, a beacon to remind us that safe harbors may yet exist where the light does not hold dominion.

Day 24: We've taken to playing a word association game in which we try to relate objects in the basement to memories from our former lives—either of which might be illusory at this point.

Day 25: One of the men in our enclave broke down today, repeatedly screaming the phrase "Extinction in green" and pounding his head against the concrete floor; though we tried to restrain him, he still managed to injure himself so severely that he lost consciousness and has remained catatonic ever since.

Day 26: This evening, after the man who beat himself senseless stopped breathing, we stuffed his body into the dryer in the laundry room and recited a liturgy of broken prayers.

Day 27: The light that seeps in from around the door seems to obey no rule of physics, twisting and turning like a snake seeking purchase on a tree limb or a tentacle sneaking toward prey.

Day 28: A terrible, low rumble like a million mountaintops collapsing in tandem has shaken our walls and bludgeoned our skulls all day.

Day 29: One of the women in our group volunteered to scout beyond the basement door, but we value companionship more than freedom at this point, so we declined the offer; time and pressure, however, may very well change our estimation of worth.

Day 30: The other man, the one who didn't beat in his head, tried to charge his phone with a bare wire and burned his hand to the muscle—proof that ingenuity born of ignorance will not save us as it did our cave-dwelling forebears.

Day 31: We have lived in the basement for one full month, but time has no relevance where cataclysm is concerned; days, months, or years cannot adequately measure the full dimensions of terror.

Day 32: The emerald light slithered farther across the floor today than it ever had before, backing us all into a corner in the rec room where we hugged one another and confessed our sins.

Day 33: We remain huddled in the now urine-soaked corner, packed tight as cattle on a killing floor and perhaps just as frightened.

Day 34: The woman who volunteered to scout beyond the basement stuck her foot into the light, where it began to contort and elongate like chewed bubble gum stretched between two fingers; she flinched away almost instantly, but her foot remains changed.

Day 35: The light finally receded to its usual orbit around the basement door and granted us a temporary stay of execution.

Day 36: Yesterday's entry may have been preemptive, as a plague of bulldozer-sized locusts—or something far more unimaginable—has chittered at an unbearable volume all day, making it impossible to hold a thought for more than a few seconds.

Day 37: The chittering abides, has increased in scope and magnitude, causes us intense nausea and uncontrollable vomiting as blood leaks from our ears.

Day 38: The insectile assault continues, the air thick with vibration and difficult to breathe; is this the mocking laughter of the light?

Day 39: Hard to concentrate through the many-legged hallucinations, the dark spots skittering at the corners of my vision, the dry heaving of pink-tinged phlegm and bile.

Day 40: Finally blessed silence has regained control and we have regained some semblance of bodily function, though we are dehydrated and starving.

Day 41: We slipped in and out of sleep all day, but during our brief bursts of awareness we saw willowy silhouettes dashing through the light on the opposite side of the door; none of us had the desire to investigate further.

Day 42: After counting the cans of food left to us and determining our current rate of consumption, we've concluded that, with tighter rationing, we can survive for approximately 120 more days if we so choose.

Day 43: A fact none of us realized until the woman who rarely speaks mentioned it: we haven't heard the patter of rain against the house's siding since we retreated to this enclave.

Day 44: On a whim, we tied a clothes hanger we found in the laundry room to a piece of string and slid it under the basement door; by the time we reeled it back a few minutes later, it had acquired a pearlescent greenish-black hue and serrated edges, transforming into an object that calls to mind alien weaponry and predatory biology.

Day 45: Neither the single pop of a gunshot nor the desperate howl of a siren has reached us in our prison, which leads us to assume that rescue is, at best, a comforting fairy tale.

Day 46: The emerald light has surely burned away everyone we loved or wished we could have loved, everyone we hated or should have hated; perhaps it burned away our capacity to ever love or hate again as well.

Day 47: The woman who volunteered to go outside stares at her misshapen foot for hours at a time then examines her opposite foot and her hands, which forces me to wonder whether she takes comfort in the normalcy of these other appendages or wishes that they, too, would be stretched into the strange new future of the world.

Day 48: The man with the burned hand proposed a theory: that beings from another realm of existence have come to terraform our galaxy and develop it in the same way construction crews develop untamed fields and virgin forests; he suggests that we are the ants populating those natural spaces and the light, with its attendant noises, is part of indifferent machinery too complex for our understanding.

Day 49: I've considered the man's theory from various angles but cannot ascribe to it for one reason: "development" as a project is a human construct and I see no reason to believe that what lies beyond the basement door has any relationship to humanity or its inconsequential motivations.

Day 50: We cry frequently, over nothing in particular and everything in general, and we laugh at inappropriate moments, like when someone bumped the ON button of the dryer and the dead man within spun head over heels for a full three minutes.

Day 51: There have been too many consecutive days without notable sounds or changes in the light's behavior; this serenity disturbs us more than the tortures we've already endured.

Day 52: We worry about the ways we will die, as all of us agree that we would prefer to meet our ends from familiar reapers like knives, guns, ropes, and drugs; none of us has the courage to mention old age or natural causes, even as vague possibilities.

Day 53: The woman who volunteered to go outside suggested we remove the basement door from its hinges and push forward, into the light, using the door as a shield—a bold plan, a desperate plan, but an untenable plan, given that the light seems to shine from every direction.

Day 54: Today, the faucet in the laundry room shuddered, moaned, and spat a gelatinous, forest green liquid that smells of freshly mowed grass and ammonia.

Day 55: Because the pipes continue to produce only the dark green ooze, we have been forced to open our stores of bottled water, which we saved for an eventuality such as this.

Day 56: Something heavy landed on the roof and moved about in rapid, seven-step jitters for part of the day; we believe it is gone now, but, for all we know, it could still be resting atop the house.

Day 57: Another observation from the woman who rarely speaks: despite the fact that we live in a basement, we have seen no mice or spiders or ants or roaches or any other common denizen of dark corners—an implausible coincidence at best.

Day 58: The light has found a way to climb the length of the ceiling; it hangs above us, threatening to fall like a final curtain and finish its work.

Day 59: We fear to stand, nervous that the light may somehow reach down and pluck us from our shaded preserve, so, instead, we have begun to crawl along the floor on hands and knees, like infants learning to navigate the intricacies of bodily motion.

Day 60: Due to our need to conserve water we have been unable to wash ourselves for almost a week, thus the stench of stagnant flesh and overheated crevices has become the better part of our atmosphere.

Day 61: The man with the burned hand pulled the billiards table across the basement and enlisted our help in flipping it on its end and propping in front of the door; he imagined that it could block the cracks along the doorframe where light sneaked in and, so far, it has.

Day 62: We woke to a tremendous crash and found the man with the burned hand crushed beneath the pool table, blood foaming from his mouth; he couldn't tell us what had happened, but he did wheeze a too-familiar phrase to us before expiring—"Extinction in green."

Day 63: We held an impromptu funeral for the man with the burned hand and shut his corpse away inside the washing machine; we didn't discuss where we will store the next one of our dead.

Day 64: We're bothered by how the man with the burned hand came to be positioned under the table and we're suspicious of the reason it tipped over; we agree that the light is responsible for both, though we cannot prove its crimes.

Day 65: Without the extra barrier of the pool table, the light has again swept across the ceiling and shines brightest above the spot where the man with the burned hand met his end, as if in mockery.

Day 66: A question I cannot help but increasingly entertain: is the light alive and self-aware?

Day 67: Our experience no longer contains the capacity for reasonable explanations; whatever happened to the world brought with it an alternative system of logic and a strange, new set of physical laws.

Day 68: The woman who volunteered to scout beyond the door spent the entire day in the laundry room, turning the faucet on and off, staring at the dark green liquid that flows from the pipes.

Day 69: For several hours, I watched the stream of liquid with the woman who volunteered to scout beyond the door; I must concede that I, too, am mesmerized by the way the liquid catches the emerald light and transforms its bruising glare into a river of impossible stars.

Day 70: It's becoming ever more difficult to remember the excited trill of birdsongs in the morning, the venerable musk of old books pulled from a dusty shelf, and the silken heat of our lovers' lips against our throats.

Day 71: For no reason we can discern, the light above us now ripples like the surface of a lake blown anxious by gusting winds.

Day 72: We continue to lie in the laundry room and gaze at the stream of liquid; occasionally, one of us will ask a rhetorical question like "What happens when our water runs out?" and expect the viridian ooze to provide an answer, but it never does.

Day 73: Today, the woman who volunteered to scout beyond the door ran her hands through the flow of dark green liquid—an action that caused her fingers to lengthen, narrow, and fuse together in a raptorial claw similar to those of mantises.

Day 74: The woman with mantis hands insists that they cause her no pain; in fact, she says that her hands feel stronger, more dexterous, and more a part of herself than ever before.

Day 75: We watched the woman with mantis hands snap a steel pipe in half with a flick of her wrist and silently considered how easily those alien hands could break a neck, a skull, or a spine.

Day 76: Is the liquid a condensed form of the light or a tool of the light or is it a medium that allows the light to be what it is?

Day 77: The woman with mantis hands decided to run her feet under the green liquid; her already elongated foot changed rapidly, gaining needle-like bristles, sharp talons, and two additional toes.

Day 78: In the woman who volunteered becoming the woman with mantis hands, we have crossed over a line that should demarcate reality from fiction but, clearly, no longer does.

Day 79: Everywhere the woman with mantis hands crawls, the light brightens above her.

Day 80: The woman with mantis hands scaled one of the basement's concrete walls and, laughing all the while, hung upon it for half the day.

Day 81: The woman who rarely speaks drew me aside and asked how long we could safely reside in the same space as the woman with mantis hands; I answered that the time for safety was already long past.

Day 82: Part of me wants to see the woman with mantis hands finish whatever metamorphosis she's begun; another part of me trembles to conceive of that metamorphosis's final result.

Day 83: Something like an air raid siren, but much deeper and hollower, echoed through the basement three times today.

Day 84: The woman with mantis hands says she's going to drink the green liquid; she says she'd rather keep changing and live than stay boxed in this basement and wither away.

Day 85: To protect ourselves, we removed the knobs from the faucet in the laundry room while the woman with mantis hands slept—a cowardly act, perhaps, but at the end of the world bravado is sibling to death.

Day 86: When the woman with mantis hands discovered the lack of knobs, she eyed us with hatred, slashed through a case of our water with one of her taloned feet, and told us that we didn't understand "what sacrifice the future demands."

Day 87: The woman with mantis hands says she is leaving tomorrow, says she has new thoughts that cannot be expressed in words, says she cannot guarantee our immunity from her rage.

Day 88: The woman with mantis hands opened the basement door, flooding emerald light over all but a sliver of laundry room, and walked out, slamming the door behind her; we expected her to shout "Extinction in green" as she left, but, instead, she said nothing, her silence a reminder of how limited our powers of communication truly are.

Day 89: Less than three months since the light arrived, and only the woman who rarely speaks and I remain.

Day 90: I hope dogs continue to survive out there, somewhere; dogs were always the best of us.

Day 91: The woman who rarely speaks drew a circle on the wall and told me that it encompassed the remainder of the known universe.

Day 92: We argued religion today, with the woman who rarely speaks exhorting me to "trust in the Lord's plan" after I suggested that there might be no God watching over us; debate ground to a halt when I pointed to the light flooding over the ceiling and shouted, "Maybe *that's* God"—a possibility too close to our most worrisome suspicions for either of us to continue debating.

Day 93: Another day, another bizarre blast of noise—this time an earthshaking buzz like a rocket powered by a hundred billion bees lifting off its launching pad.

Day 94: The light creeped down the walls a few inches; even on our hands and knees, we no longer feel out of reach.

Day 95: The woman who rarely speaks told me a story about her five year old son and his first day of kindergarten—how nervous he was, how nervous she was, how letting go felt both entirely wrong but absolutely right, how his face lit up when he stepped off the bus and saw her at the end of the day, and how his face lit up when he talked about his teacher and all the new friends he'd made at school; she says she hopes he's found new friends again, wherever he is.

Day 96: I miss my husband, my dogs, my parents, and my friends; I miss the excited rush of wind against my face just before a thunderstorm and the bite of a freshly brewed cup of coffee in the morning; I miss not feeling scared every moment of my life.

Day 97: The light has pulled itself a few inches lower, so that if we did walk upright, it would graze the tops of our heads.

Day 98: If memory serves, today should be the first day of winter, yet the temperature in the basement hasn't dropped even a few degrees from when we first arrived.

Day 99: The woman who rarely speaks gathered the remaining food and water into a single pile and fell asleep atop it.

Day 100: Should we mark this centenary with song and dance or a memorial service?

Day 101: I tossed one of the billiards balls up, into the light above us, to gauge how quickly the light worked its transformation; it fell back into my hand as a deep green, metallic disk.

Day 102: The woman who rarely speaks is counting and recounting every last article of sustenance we possess; she hugs each can and bottle to her chest as she numbers it and gently stacks it among others of its kind.

Day 103: I've been thinking a great deal about the woman with mantis hands and the wonders and horrors she might be seeing now, if she is still alive; I find myself almost yearning to see them, too, if for no other reason than to break the monotony of the cinder block cavern that surrounds me.

Day 104: The light dropped further today and now nearly touches our backs when we skitter about on all fours.

Day 105: We have taken to lying flat and unmoving, so as to not draw the light's attention.

Day 106: We squirm along the floor like awkward grub worms when we need water, food, and bathroom breaks; otherwise, we lie in our makeshift beds and let our minds drift to the edge of sanity.

Day 107: This is not a life we're leading; this is a form of death no one knew existed.

Day 108: Maybe I'm letting abstract thought run away with me, but I'm beginning to wonder if the light is a mode of evolution rather than extinction—and I'm also beginning to wonder if, in this instance, there's any difference between the two.

Day 109: Transformation is the keystone of the universe, and yet it's an unsettling concept for creatures such as ourselves, who cling tight to the notion of an unwavering essence at our cores.

Day 110: Apropos of our current situation, I recall one of my college philosophy professors remarking: "A thing has to stop *being* in order to *become*."

Day 111: I'm increasingly tempted to stand up and let the light burn my face into a new tomorrow.

Day 112: The woman who rarely speaks coos to individual cans of beans and jars of peanut butter as though they were pets or children.

Day 113: Chittering again today, but different this time—less raucous and more patterned, like speech from a mouth that cannot form human sound.

Day 114: The light gathered itself in a great wave and rolled over the pile of food and water the woman who rarely speaks assembled; she moved in time to be unaffected, but all our rations have mutated.

Day 115: Already, after only a day without sustenance, my head throbs from dehydration and my fingers shake with hunger. Our water has turned viscous and dark green, like the liquid from the pipes, and the canned goods have reshaped themselves into strange configurations that resemble squat bacteriophages. Within the cans, we've found translucent pastes that smell of copper, gelatinous ochre mounds that hiss when exposed to air, tiny spheres dark as midnight, and a fuzzy substance of many hues that swirls clockwise even when it's untouched. If this is water and food, it is not for us. At least, not yet.

The woman who rarely speaks is curled on the floor, chanting "We'll be fine." I tried to talk to her, to plan an escape, but she didn't respond. I believe she intends to stay in the basement and wait for miracles. I believe she will die.

As for the light, after transforming our supplies it retracted to its pool on the ceiling. There it remains, rippling contentedly.

I realize this entry is overlong, but surely there cannot be many more to come.

Day 116: I've made a decision, and the decision is mine alone. I will walk out of the basement, into the emerald light. The woman who rarely speaks can't be moved, though I've tried. Balled up in a fetal position, she's entered an unresponsive reverie. She whispers to herself a phrase that sounds too much like "Extinction in green" and whenever I touch her, she thrashes violently, as if in full seizure. I have no medical background, no psychiatric training, so I let her be.

I assume that when I enter the light something will happen to me. Maybe my flesh will grow sleek and hard and powerful. Maybe I will acquire new senses that reveal so much more of the world. Or maybe I will simply crumble under the light's intensity and there will be no more "me" to worry about my fate.

Whatever the case, this is the only option. I must go.

Day 117: Last entry. Vision spins. Stomach feels torn in two. It's now or never.

I hope I find my husband.

I hope I can breathe fresh air again.

I'm excited.

I'm terrified.

I'm tired of being.

I'm ready to become.

Etch the Unthinkable

THE THEATER WAS located in a long-abandoned warehouse on the outskirts of the city. Roof partially collapsed, windows mostly broken, and walls covered in thick, dark mounds of unidentifiable lichen and fungus, it seemed an unlikely place for a comedy show. And yet, despite this unlikelihood (or maybe because of it), the queue to enter stretched halfway around the moldering structure.

Every person who waited in line held two items: a rusted token with a pair of falcon wings imprinted on both sides and a one-gallon container filled with gasoline. These would-be patrons chatted with one another in brief, excited blurbs, their eyes glistening with desperate hope. A great deal of nervous laughter punctuated the evening sky and phrases such as "I always thought Etch was an urban legend," "Do you think he can do it?" and "Can a clown really be *that* funny?" floated up from the murmuring throng.

As dusk retreated before night's swift blade, the warehouse doors swung open and the conversations quieted to barely whispered confessions and epithets. Gravity pulled harder, and a litany of scourges filled the air. "Cancer," "Alzheimer's," "ALS," "depression": these were the words that suddenly crowded out the laughter and anticipation that had hung like colorful balloons above the old industrial building only moments before; they strangled the firmament and burst every floating joy to make room for themselves. Even the very stars above began to ache and roil with diseased sufferings.

The line began to inch forward.

Movement made what lay within the warehouse more than possibility, more than dream. It meant that Etch would perform. It meant that everything told in fables and fairy tales might be true. It meant that monsters did, indeed, hide under the bed and inside the closet.

When the audience began to shuffle toward the entrance, many people peeled off into the night, rushing back to their cars, their homes, their families. Later, palms still sweaty, legs still shaking, they'd face the same infirmities that drove them to seek out the show in the first place, and they'd reconsider their decision. They'd claw and they'd scrape and they'd try to win their battles on their own, but, inevitably, they would be overrun by the insatiable masses that had accumulated within them. To their last breath, these stragglers would try to imagine, in vain, what it might have been like to be in Etch's gallery and partake of his show. Eyes sunken and muscles withered, they'd try to picture themselves inside the makeshift theater. They'd try to conjure the jokes and skits and pratfalls, but none would be right. They'd dream of Etch's face, but Etch had no face like they'd ever seen. They'd think often of the others, the ones who'd gone on without them, who'd chanced the meeting with Etch. When their time came, it is true that they would die in as much safety as death can afford: in their own beds, with their families nearby, without sensation and without illumination. And yet, even so, even in their placid demises, they would remain discontented and ever wondering for reasons they understood too well.

Such was the future of those who broke from the line.

The people who remained, however, discovered an entirely different fate. Hands trembling and legs weak, they passed into the warehouse where a pair of naked doormen greeted their arrival. The doormen, unclothed but for paper bags with smiley faces drawn upon them that they wore over their heads, collected the tokens from the entrants and directed them to a series of patio tables and rickety plastic chairs. Here the audience members waited in silence. No one dared speak, for speech would have invited recognition, and in this place, no one wanted to be acknowledged for the choice they'd made.

Instead, all sets of eyes were pasted to the center of the abandoned warehouse floor, upon which stretched a wide, ramshackle stage composed of loose wooden planks arranged atop a series of sawhorses. Two poles stood at either end of the stage, with a clothesline strung between them. On the taut line hung a wide swath of red velvet with a strange helical sigil stitched across its surface. The entire panorama was lit by two candelabras set at opposing sides of the makeshift curtain.

Once everyone in the audience had slid into their seats, the bagmen-ushers closed the doors and chained them shut, clicking in place a series of heavy padlocks so that further entrance—or exit—would be impossible. The anticipation in the room swelled, and so too did a tang of sweat spread throughout the warehouse, its scent growing sharp and unforgiving as a surgeon's scalpel.

After what seemed like several lifetimes, a figure emerged from under the curtain. A round, noseless face, glowing pale in the guttering light. Unpainted, diamond-shaped eyes without irises, dark as the edge of the universe. A toothless, frozen grin, too wide, much too wide, ringed not in red but in a shimmering, nameless color almost beyond human ken. And, within a black and white polka dotted jumpsuit, joints, too many joints, all bending at uncanny, marionette angles.

Etch the Clown. Etch the Unthinkable.

In silence, the audience stirred, recoiled. They'd not anticipated this *thing*, not even with all the legends they'd heard, the midnight tales told over campfires and crackling hearths. Fear rolled over the warehouse. Someone stood and knocked over a table, which rattled against the floor.

Etch cocked his head to the side, grin unwavering, eyes unblinking. His body contorted like a spider about to leap upon its prey.

A chair squealed against cement as it was pushed back. The audience tensed, most readying for flight.

But Etch did not leap from his stage. Instead, he folded in upon himself, an impossible Gordian knot of limbs, and rolled to one side of the stage, then unfolded and stood. He gazed upon his audience, his head again cocked to the side and performed what could only be called a grotesque jig.

In the audience, muscles ached. Hands trembled. Flight was still a very real possibility. Fear was still heavy in the atmosphere.

And then, from a distant world on the outskirts of sanity and reason, a laugh—the first drop of rain from an impending hurricane.

One laugh grew to two, two to four, and four to eight. Soon, every member of the audience rocked in their seats, on their feet, on the floor. They couldn't understand why they laughed. If they thought about it—and thought was becoming ever more difficult—they could find no real trigger for their laughter other than Etch's horrifying jig. Yet they couldn't contain it. In truth, they didn't want to contain it. And so, laughter swept through the warehouse, shook its foundations; it tore at the sinews of throats, at the linings of lungs, drowning every care, every thought, every emotion.

Etch again folded in upon himself, rolled to the opposite end of the stage, unfolded, and danced.

The laughter grew more unhinged, less the noise from an audience than a madhouse.

Etch watched, head tilted, eyes unblinking, grin always too wide.

On and on it went. Etch becoming infinitely recursive, performing his macabre dance at one end of the stage then the other, and the people in the audience laughing louder, laughing as they never had, so hard, so long, without so much reason.

The laughter did not stop, could not stop. It continued to grow wildly, all out of proportion to the vessels through which it flowed. It strained bodies to their breaking points, blotting out pain and horror with a maniacal glee. It crashed through flesh, through minds, consuming all in its path. Jaws cracked and splintered. Larynges shredded like tissue paper. Lungs burst. Hearts sputtered and stopped.

One by one, the members of the audience surrendered to the insatiable laughter and slipped away into the absurdity of it all, blood foaming from their gaping smiles. One by one, they dropped to the floor or slouched cold and limp in their seats.

Gradually, the volume diminished and Etch ceased his metronome motion. He stood at the head of a satisfied crowd, his inscrutable grin never wavering, his eyes ever impassive and searching.

When, near dawn, stillness and silence fell final, the bagmen ushers grabbed the gasoline containers that sat atop every table and poured their contents over the audience. They flipped the candelabras onto the warehouse floor, mounted the stage, and linked arms with Etch, whose arachnid reach drew them to himself, into himself, through himself. A point of searing white light formed at his chest and he squeezed the bagmen into it, their forms impossibly stretched and flattened like wet clay.

Flames quickly overtook the warehouse.

The stage began to burn, Etch's backdrop going up like a phoenix eager for rebirth.

His grin still implacable, insatiable, Etch bowed to the dead room, then contorted and folded himself into the bright point at the center of his chest, disappearing into the harsh luster.

The flames roared in applause.

The show had ended.

The laughter, however, would go ever, ever on.

Apocalypse, Ignored

As I SCRAWL the final flourish on the Old Man's mark and step back from the abandoned office building, a police siren gives its cursory squawk—a presumptuous noise that's supposed to make you drop to your knees and surrender your will, but, frankly, just makes me despair for the state of humanity and its illusions of control. Even so, I throw my hands in the air and turn toward the patrol car behind me, its emergency lights now cutting red and blue framed shadows from the darkness.

The passenger's side window lowers, and, from the glowing interior, I hear a voice complain, "It's just a crazy homeless guy. Look at that beard."

I sidle up to the car and wave, my tattered coat flapping behind me. A youngish officer riding shotgun leans into view and motions for me to stop. His name badge, glinting gold, reads CEPEDA.

I stop immediately, lest this situation escalate.

"Sir, you're not allowed to loiter on the street after hours," the young cop says. "I'm going to have to ask you to move along."

I nod and salute, trying to shove as much faux earnestness into my voice as possible. "Will do, officer. I was on my way home right now. I had some important business I had to take care of first."

The driver laughs—a bitter sound of derision, cutting as a buzzsaw—and the youngish officer, Cepeda, cracks a patronizing smile.

"I'm sure it was *very* important business," he says, window already sliding closed. "But it's done now, right? So I don't want to see you out here when we cruise through later tonight. That's all I care about."

I nod again, click my heels together, and take off walking, though I have no particular destination in mind.

The police car rolls past me, turns the next block up, and is gone. Once I'm sure I'm out of sight, I rush back to the office building and press my ear against its outer wall. Between the atoms of the bricks, within hidden dimensions of the mortar, I hear a distant screech that could issue from no earthly creature. Innumerable appendages that remain nameless in our world thrash within those bricks. I smile and kiss the Old Man's mark, the glyph I scratched on the wall not even ten minutes before, the glyph that's branded my blood.

The Things are blocked—for the time being, at least—but I already feel them whirring through their netherspace, seeking another fissure through which they might gain entrance. It's time to move. It's always time to move.

Those cops don't need to worry; I won't be here later. I'll be making sure *they're* safe. I'll be tracking the Things as best I can. Without a home to call my own, without a penny to my inconsequential name, without a single handshake of thanks, I'll be saving the world the same as I do every minute of every day and every night. And they'll laugh at me for it. They'll deride me. They'll tell me to get a job and get off the street. But I'll be saving their asses all the same. I'm living an apocalypse, ignored, and no one cares.

I know what people see when they speed by me: a weather-beaten lunatic. My clothes—the gray pajama suit and black overcoat I was wearing so many years ago when my battle against the Things began—are caked in a layer of mud and grime and viscous substances I'd rather not consider. Complement the ratty attire with my visage—sunken cheeks, unkempt hair, and a beard to rival a Viking lord—and I frighten people. They blast past me and purposefully avert their gazes. I know that they're scared. It's not so much that I might be hiding a shiv in my boot or that I might be planning to shank them and take their cash and their lives; no, it's that whatever's wrong with me, whatever caused me to end up on the streets and turn into a tattered shade of a person, might be communicable to them through my eyes alone.

I can understand the sentiment. I used to feel the same way. Long ago, I drove a BMW. I slept under Egyptian linen sheets. I stared at my watch, at my phone, at the sky or the upholstery of my car, just so I didn't have to meet the suicide stares of people holding signs that read "Unemployed Father of Three. Anything Helps. God Bless," "Hungry. Need Food. Willing to Work. Please Help," or "Homeless Vet. Can't Find Job. America 4 Ever." Somehow, even then, I knew—I think we all know, whether we like to admit it or not—that the thinnest of threads separate "us" from "them," and that any day, for any reason, those threads can snap, and we can go tumbling down into poverty's heavy dust.

So, yeah, I know what people see when they pass me by. They see a plague carrier, a walking virus, a man who might activate some dormant pathogen of failure within themselves. Too bad they don't understand where the real infection lies.

As I stroll along the avenues that form the uneasy nexus between urban decay and suburban ignorance, I feel for the miasmic trail of the Things. They're moving. They're scouting. And, inevitably, as they always do, they're trying to find another malleable wall between their reality and ours, another ruined place thick with the lingering fumes of despair and abandonment.

I follow their ethereal slime deeper into the suburbs, the streetlights glowing brighter here. My fingertips tingle. Something is awry. The Things are too far from their normal hunting grounds. A couple years ago, when the housing bubble burst, they tried to breach some foreclosed homes in the outer neighborhoods, but, generally, the Things don't wander too far from the tenements and shadow streets and crumbling warehouses of the city's inner ring. If they're sliding this far into the land of white picket fences, they must have found an extremely weak point, which is bad. Very bad. It means they might have a shot at breaking through. It means the past is returning to me.

I quicken my step and try to slink from shadow to shadow unnoticed. Chasing the Things beyond the city's inner ring entails certain dangers. After all, disheveled, homeless men tend to receive chilly receptions when, in the lumbering hours of the night, they wander through neighborhoods where the average house value tops three hundred thousand dollars. If the wrong person spots me and I don't hide fast enough, I'll be spending a lot more time with the cops, guaranteed.

Some college-aged kids in an SUV roll up beside me, shout "Loser," and wing a half-empty beer can toward my head. It clangs off the sidewalk and bounces into the street. The SUV peels out, rocketing down the road to a distant stoplight. A stream of hyena howls follows in its wake.

"Morons," I sigh. For a moment, I consider turning around and letting the Things ravage this burg, this nation, this planet. But a plastic tricycle sitting abandoned in the middle of a nearby yard spurs me on.

My daughter would have been twelve this year. My wife would have turned forty-three. They still age in my heart. But in my mind, they're frozen mid-scream eight years ago, eternally wrapped in dark, diaphanous folds and pierced by pitch black tetrahedrons.

My hatred of the Things suddenly renewed, I spread my senses wider and pick up my pace. There's nothing like vengeance to keep the fire of a man's soul burning clean and pure.

Somewhere nearby I can already feel what the Things feel—an erosion in the fabric of space and time.

Following the taut, vibrating bands of the universe, I arrive at a renovated Craftsman-style house decked out in sky blue and white. It's fronted by a neatly trimmed hedgerow and a well-manicured lawn that contains two portrait-worthy oak trees. Every window is darkened at this late hour, as is considered good and proper, and two ornate, wrought iron lamps glow silver on either side of the front door. There's even a tire swing hanging from one of the oaks, for godssake. The property is an evangelist for family values, American values, the conquest of a homogenized peace and prosperity over the natural order of all things. But I know that inside something has grinded reality to the bone. This Norman Rockwell territory has been annexed by David Lynch. Most people just can't see the transition of power, hidden behind the world as it is.

The Things won't wait long, so neither can I. Risking what I have to risk, I stride over the plush lawn and stand before the house's front door. Beneath my feet, the doormat proclaims a bold "Welcome Friends." Somehow, I doubt it's speaking to me.

I crouch and lift up the mat, then pull out a Sharpie and draw the mark of the Old Man. Alone, it's not enough to bar the Things from entering. Not with space-time as thin as it is here. But if I can get inside and scrawl a few more sigils, maybe carve a couple into the house's studs or support beams, I might be able to hold them at bay.

I rise to hit the doorbell button and let the mat flop back into place. A vaguely ominous chime—not unlike the peal of a lone church bell—rings, muted, from within the house. I wait.

This all seems too full circle, too déjà vu. I remember my own doorbell eight years past. I remember the crazy, wild-eyed Old Man jittering on my porch. And I remember the cries from upstairs, from the bedrooms, that set both me and the old man blazing to the second floor.

No one answers, so I mash on the button again.

Again, no answer.

The Things are gathering under the surface of this American dream. I can feel the pressure of their numbers between subatomic particles.

I pound on the surprisingly sturdy door and shout, "Listen, I know what you're thinking. You're thinking there's a crazy vagrant out here who wants you to open up so he can run you through with a switchblade and rob you blind. But that's not the case. I only want a glass of water. Just a glass of water. Please."

Voices—harried voices—scuttle behind the door. Finally, a response. I draw my face into the most personable smile I can manage and smooth down my hair. I think I'm steeled for what's sure to be an uncomfortable meet and greet when, all at once, a light flashes on, the door flies open, and a gangly man in a puffy blue bathrobe that reminds me of medieval royal vestments appears in the doorway, a pistol in his hand leveled directly at my head. Over his shoulder, beyond the threshold, I spy a pale, diminutive specter of a woman and, behind her, two shadow halflings—children, I presume.

"There's nothing for you here," the man growls. "There's nothing for anyone here. So keep moving along."

I raise my palms in surrender. "Whoa. Sir. Relax. I don't mean any harm. I don't have anywhere to go, and I'm dying of thirst out here. It's a hot night. If I could just come inside and have a glass of water."

The man stabs the pistol toward me and yells, "I won't tell you again. Go. Now. We've already called the police. There doesn't have to be more trouble."

I take a furtive step forward. Pressure builds in the quantum alluvium of reality. My lungs feel as drained and aching as they do in the warning hours just before an infection erupts in a geyser of fever, chills, and exhaustion. The Things are beneath us, above us, around us, inside us. They are a virus ever drifting within the cosmic body.

"Sir," I say, "Please. I know you're experiencing some difficulties. A lost job. A bankruptcy. A death in the family. I don't know exactly what your problems are, but we all have them. I'm just looking for a warm room and some water—even if it's only for a couple minutes."

The gun wavers, drops an inch.

I hit on one of the issues. Whatever plagues this family is serious—so serious that their collective worry and frustration and desperation have scoured thin the substance of the world.

"Don't. Don't you come any closer. You don't know anything." Another warning, but far weaker than the first two.

Risking the bullet, I take another step.

"Sir, please. I'll stand in the foyer. All I ask is one glass. One glass of water and I'll be on my way."

I could charge in and bowl over these people, but I'd rather they let me in their house of their own accord. I need to draw the sigils on the walls and mark each of the family members in turn, all of which will be quite a bit more difficult if they perceive me as a violent intruder.

I move in closer, close enough to see the man's eyes. Something's wrong with them. They're wavering and rippling, like water in the wake of a mighty sea serpent.

"We just... we can't. You need to leave." he says, pistol dropping another inch.

I'm losing patience here. I wonder if I was this callous and ignorant when the Old Man came to my door. I certainly didn't welcome him with rose petals and red carpets. I didn't even bother looking him in the eye. I was too frightened that I might have seen a part of myself looking back, that the haggard spirit beneath my skin had somehow shucked me and dressed itself in flesh all its own.

The woman standing behind the man grabs his shoulder and pulls him backward. "Honey," she says, "Close the door. And lock it. The police will be here soon. We don't have to deal with this."

I can't let that door click shut. If I don't enter the house, if I don't inscribe the Old Man's mark on these people and their ruined world... well, I'd rather not relive my own memories.

I take one more step toward the family and the door begins to swing closed, the woman herding her children and her husband away from the crazy vagabond on the street. They're prepared to barricade themselves away inside their all-American nightmare to escape me. So I do what I know is stupid, what I know I shouldn't do, what I have no other choice to do. I lunge at the doorway.

Three things happen simultaneously.

First, the street bursts into alternating shades of fire and ice.

Second, the crack of a bullet erupts from the man's handgun.

And third, the air around the house begins to vibrate as though some trickster god has struck a monstrous tuning fork and is holding it just above our heads.

I find myself suddenly lying on my back, and I'm not entirely sure why. I try to roll over, but a lance of sharp, burning pain thrusts itself through my left shoulder. Behind me, I hear shouting. Someone yells something about a gun. Someone else yells something about a perp. Inside the house, the kids are screaming; the wife is crying "Mike, what did you do? What did you do?"

I have to get on my feet. Reality is rippling like a flag in a hurricane. It won't be long until the Things tear through. Minutes, if I'm lucky. Seconds, if I'm not.

I raise a hand to my shoulder and feel warm, viscid liquid on my fingers. It dawns on me: I've been shot. I've never taken a bullet until tonight. Been shot *at* a couple times, sure. Anyone who lives on the street long enough is bound to be. But I've never actually *been* shot. Until now.

"Sir, put the weapon on the ground," a familiar voice rings out, and I look up to see the young officer from earlier this evening—CEPEDA—standing over me. He goes down on one knee as his partner chugs toward the house.

Without meeting my eyes, Cepeda examines my wound and radios for an ambulance. I roll onto my uninjured side and push myself up, onto my knees.

"Sir," Cepeda says, a palm suddenly on my injured shoulder, "stay down. Paramedics will be here in just a couple minutes."

I try to rise, but the kid's grip tightens. A drill of pain blasts me back to my knees.

I swallow a wave of nausea and stare up at my captor. "We don't have that long. They're coming. Can you feel it?"

He finally looks at my face. He remembers me. I know. He knows. His mouth opens, as though to say something, to give me the recognition of personhood, but instead he glances away and mumbles, "Just stay down."

The layers of reality here are oscillating so rapidly that I can no longer see the house or the people standing in its open doorway. I've only witnessed a vibration this violent once before—the night my family died, the night the Old Man arrived, the night I had to take up this mantle.

"Listen to me," I say, trying to remain calm. "If you don't let me up, something indescribably terrible is going to happen. I'm not psychotic. I'm not on drugs. But I have to get inside that house. I don't want to steal anything. I don't want to hurt the family. I don't even want to stay for more than a couple minutes. I just have to write a few things. Inside the house."

Without warning, the air around us goes cold. Polar cold. Deep space cold. Gooseflesh rises on Cepeda's uncovered arms. I think I see frost on his gun and his badge. "What the hell?" he whispers, his question breathed out as a cloud of fog.

Again, I try to stand and this time Cepeda doesn't stop me. He's too shocked, too disconcerted. I stagger and sway but manage to remain upright.

"You don't want to know where that chill came from," I say, "but far worse things are going to follow after it unless we go inside that house."

Eyes darting between me and the house, Cepeda rests the tips of his fingers on his holstered gun.

"It's just a breeze," he says, desperate for a rational answer. "Wind gets cold off the bay at night."

The house has become nothing but a blur of colors, its edges leaking out into the yard, where even the hedges and the grass begin to waver and dissipate.

I can't let this happen. I have a duty, an oath to uphold. I have a promise to keep to my family and the Old Man. But I also have a hole in my shoulder and a police guard who's nervous enough to give me another one in the chest if I make any sudden moves.

While I consider how well Cepeda might be able to aim, the first scream erupts from the house. It's a little girl's scream, and my blood recoils from it, throwing me eight years into the past, to a night too much like tonight, to a night I should have died but was reborn in a gutter.

The little girl is still screaming, only it's my daughter, Ally. I'm standing in the half-darkened doorway of our empty house with my fingers clenched around the Old Man's arm. The doormat beneath the Old Man still reads "THE WIRTHS" even though the people from the bank are coming by tomorrow to make sure we've vacated.

Ally's scream causes me to whirl around and inadvertently drag the old guy inside with me, which is where he wanted to be all along. Nichole, my wife, pounces upstairs like the graceful tigress she is, and I turn my attention to the Old Man, who's struggling to free himself from my grip. In better light, he resembles a gaunt, war-weary Morgan Freeman.

Ally screams again and this time Nichole joins in harmony.

"Les!" she cries out. "Lester!"

The house suddenly feels as though it's been thrust beneath a glacier.

"What the hell is going on?" I ask the Old Man, throwing him against the foyer wall. He doesn't answer, he just moves—faster than I'd imagined he could—in pursuit of the fear.

He's hustling up the stairs, taking three at a time, and I follow suit.

Another scream echoes from the bedroom hallway and Nichole flies to the head of the stairs, dragging Ally in tow. And that's when I see one of the Things for the very first time, trailing at the heels of my daughter.

Featureless inverted pyramid-shaped head carved from glistening onyx; body composed of nothing more than a thin, tight coil that dangles beneath the head; appendages that unwind from the end of the coil to form a mass of undulating filament-tendrils—this is what I see, and the worst part is that it levitates off the ground, so all I can think is that this Thing, whatever it is, doesn't just look like a virus grown to the size of a human, it also defies all conceptions of physics. The absolute *wrongness* of the Thing in refusing to adhere to my safe, little, universal laws freezes me on the stairs. It makes me shrink in terror, in dread. And my moment of hesitation costs me everything that still matters.

Back in the present, I don't hesitate. I know what has to be done. I rocket toward the blur of the house and Cepeda doesn't stop me. Instead, he follows, pistol drawn.

The little girl screams again, and a series of gun shots peel away the neighborhood's quiet composure. I can only imagine that eyes are beginning to leer through curtain cracks up and down the street.

I rush through the front doorway and nearly bowl over the little girl. She's planted herself on the threshold and is staring into an adjoining room, some sort of purple stuffed animal crushed to her chest. I follow her gaze to a cozy den lined with puffy couches, an inordinately complex entertainment system, and arcs of blood spray. The man who shot me lies in the middle of the floor, his face in pieces. Cepeda's partner hangs over the man as though he's suspended on a wire. The shining black tip of one of the Things' heads protrudes from a gaping slit in the cop's stomach.

The Thing that's impaled the officer whips its head to the side and half the policeman's body goes flying toward the wall, hitting it with a crunch and a wet thud. The other half collapses to the floor.

At the far end of the room, the woman from the doorway and a little boy hunch in a corner, desperate to remain inconspicuous though they're both crying with their hands latched tight upon their mouths. No chance they won't be noticed. The Thing's tendrils are already rippling in their direction. It could've sensed their misery three universes away.

Cepeda shoulders past me and fires off two shots at the Thing, but the bullets simply enter its upside-down pyramid head and vanish without even lightly chipping the glassy surface. The shots do command the Thing's attention, though. Its filaments retract and wrap around its base spindle like streamers on a maypole.

"No," I shout to Cepeda. "You can't destroy it. You can only ward against it and drive it back."

"Back where?" Cepeda asks, his gun still trained on the Thing, his eyes darting between the woman and the boy and the distance he'd have to cross to reach them.

"To where they come from," I say, wiping a broad streak of my blood on the little girl's forehead before sidling up next to him.

As if on cue, another Thing floats into view from the deep shadow that looms omnipresent in the rooms beyond us.

I step toward the Things and motion for Cepeda to follow. "Stay close," I say. "Really close."

Gritting my teeth against the impending pain, I sink two fingers into the bullet wound in my shoulder and come away with a hand slicked by fresh, wine-dark blood. I brandish my fingers like knives, slashing and thrusting toward the Thing as I stride into the den. Cepeda's at my back. I can feel him using me as a shield, which, in too many ways, I am.

The Thing slowly floats backward until it bumps up against the Thing behind it. As we move closer to the woman and the boy, the fire and ice of the police car lights reflects from the room adjacent to the den and my heart nearly stops. The entire space glitters with the shiny heads of Things. More than a dozen of them hover in the darkness, their tendrils oscillating so gently, so patiently, that nothing could speak menace with more volume.

I glance over my shoulder, and Cepeda is helping the woman and boy to their feet. I paint streaks of blood on their foreheads, too, then swipe the air in front of me to keep the Things at bay. Cepeda rushes the family out of the house, which is exactly what I'd hoped he'd do.

So now there's only one more act left to perform. I knew it when I saw this place. I knew it when the vibration was so strong.

Cepeda returns, gun still drawn. I turn to him, and he's staring over my shoulder wild-eyed. He can see the number of Things we're dealing with. I lock eyes with the young officer.

"I need a couple things from you, Cepeda. You can't say 'no' to any of them or this place, right here, is where the end of the world begins."

The kid looks like the proverbial deer in headlights, only the car that's bearing down on him is never going to veer; it's just going to move at a glacial pace, roaring closer and closer until one day it grazes him—a pinprick nudge with cyclone force—and bursts him to pieces.

He nods, and I see myself eight years ago, nodding assent to the same terrible burden.

"First, I need you to shoot me in the leg. Hit the femoral. We need a lot of blood. Then I need you to wait for me to bleed. I'll take off my pants when they've sopped up most of it. You have to go outside and use that blood to make a circle around the house, on the lawn. One nice, thick streak should do it. Make sure it's unbroken. And last..."

I hesitate. This is the gut punch. This is where it all hangs in the balance.

"Last, I need you to open your mouth and stick out your tongue."

"What?" Cepeda asks, and shuffles backward an almost imperceptible inch.

"We don't have time to get into the metaphysics. Look, I need to lose buckets of blood. I probably won't make it out of here. But someone has to be on the street, twenty-four seven, keeping the Things away. That's going to have to be you. You'll never not be protecting and serving. *Really* protecting and serving. But you'll also be dragged through hell.

"You'll never receive a medal or a handshake from a mayor, even though you'll save the world every single day. See, suffering causes wounds in space-time, and wherever there's a really nasty gash—which, in a city this size, is around every corner—you'll be there, preventing an infection."

"By... by those things?" Cepeda asks, pointing at the waiting Things.

"Yeah, by those Things."

After a moment and a shellshocked "Okay," Cepeda opens his mouth wide. I dip a finger into my wound as though it's an inkwell and scrawl the mark of the Old Man on the kid's tongue.

"Swallow," I say, and he does, surprised at himself.

"In a couple days, your blood will be like mine. You'll be able to sense where the Things are. You'll feel the interconnectedness of it all. You'll realize... well... you'll see."

I turn back to the proliferation of Things in the next room. They're planning a foolproof route of escape. They have to be contained *now*.

"Shoot me," I say. "Quick."

I don't steel myself for the impact. The force sends me toppling over, onto the floor.

My leg is aflame with pain, and I see dark spots and bright spots flashing in alternate patterns all about me. Seconds shed from my life, minutes, years, decades. I glance down and my pants are soaked in blood. With what little energy I have left, I wriggle out of them and hand them to Cepeda.

"Go," I gasp. "Don't let the suffering win."

Cepeda leans down, as though he wants to say something or ask me something, but decides, instead, to merely squeeze my uninjured shoulder.

"Go," I say again, and he bolts from the den, off to his own tragic journey.

World crackling with more cold than I've ever felt, I heave myself to my feet and dip my hands into the river of blood flowing from my leg.

I think of my daughter. I think of my wife. I think of all the people outside this house. And then I charge, bloody palms outraised.

The Things try to flee, but as soon as my blood touches them, their glittering heads begin to hiss and corrode. They encircle me and whip me with their flagella, but I keep coming and touching. Just touching. That's all it takes to destroy them.

My vision grows darker, my view narrowed to a tunnel. I'm beaten, pounded, flensed, scourged.

I continue bleeding.

I continue touching.

Somewhere, far away, I hear the moan of an ambulance siren. Somewhere a little closer I hear my wife and my daughter calling my name. A name no one else will ever know. A name no one else will ever care enough to say. A name unknown.

Shale Creek

Most travelers who pass through the tiny, rural village of Shale Creek, Pennsylvania pay it no mind. With its one stoplight, two-pump gas station, and three weathered churches, it does little to provoke much outside interest. Though some people may comment on the densely forested mountains that hem in the town or the crystalline water that bubbles in the Shale Creek itself, they do not discuss these features at any length or with any real enthusiasm, and, before long, their impressions of the place fade to a few wisps of color and shadow. Inevitably, a journey through Shale Creek becomes just that: a journey *through*, to destinations worthy of being designated as destinations. That the village remains draped in the barest cloth of memory is perhaps not surprising, however. After all, it contains a bizarre secret that seems to parallel its forgotten nature. This secret? Quite simply, that no one who lived in Shale Creek between August 2016 and August 2018 can remember anything about that span of time.

On first glance, this fact may not seem particularly noteworthy. Everyone forgets. Indeed, a skeptical observer might suggest that few of us hold memories as discrete blocks of time. Instead, we mark the passage of our lives by events both wonderful and terrible, extraordinary, and unusual, and unless an event of particular importance or strangeness occurs on a given day, that day tends to be buried and broken down in the deep soil of memory. It blends with all other days and forms a foundation of unexamined normalcy from which our daily routines spring. An argument stands, therefore, that the people of Shale Creek, as a whole, may have merely experienced a span of time in which nothing notable happened to anyone. Despite its extreme improbability, such a conclusion might be somewhat satisfactory—and maybe even true—were it not for innumerable unsettling discoveries the villagers have made that imply anything but the normal occurred in Shale Creek during those two unremembered years.

Among these discoveries is the oddly shaped metal building that sits on the edge of town. In pictures from as recently as July of 2016, nothing but oak trees and crabgrass inhabited the space where the structure currently stands. The property's owner, one James Peters, a local auto mechanic who purchased the undeveloped land in 2008 with the hope of opening a shop upon it, claims that he never improved the lot due to financial problems. He cannot recall authorizing any structure to be built on the property, either, let alone building any structure there himself. Even state and county government offices have no record of the thing. Yet the structure exists.

Forty-five feet high and fashioned from what appears to be burnished gold but definitely isn't, the inverted T-shaped building displays no joints where metal plates may have been welded together nor does it reveal any evidence of rivets or bolts that might fortify the edifice. It contains no windows nor air ducts and only one heavy, oval door that no one has been able to open through either finesse or force. No noises issue from the building—in fact, the world seems to grow mute as one approaches the structure—nor has anyone ever seen a person enter or leave it. Occasionally, someone will say they smell an aroma of smoked meat wafting off the structure, but the source of such odor can never be identified. The entire building, impenetrable and of unknown use and fabrication, evokes among the people of Shale Creek a whisper of clandestine government experiments and otherworldly contact.

Whether or not the building contains anything out of the ordinary, the mere possibility of what might lie within its walls disturbs the village's residents. They imagine swirling clouds of toxic gasses no scientist can identify, dismembered torsos hanging from rusted hooks, and hostile aliens stacked neatly in a bank of time-released cryopods. They don't know why they imagine these horrors lurking inside the building when it could just as easily be filled with gold coins or chocolate cake donuts or plush unicorns. Certainly, the good people of Shale Creek don't want to imagine only fearful prospects. But something about the structure compels them to paranoid speculation. They cannot look at it without worry, without wanting to fence it in behind barbed wire, without itching for a weapon to be ready in their hands. They want to dismantle the building and send it off for scrap. They want to crush it into cubes and bury those remnants deep in an earthen pit. But they can't. No welding tool or diamond-tipped saw has made the slightest scratch on its surface. No acid has eroded its veneer. No backhoe or bulldozer has so much as dented the structure's golden exoskeleton. And so, the citizens of Shale Creek have accepted it, the way one accepts a scar. The building remains because it cannot be removed, because it is now a part of Shale Creek. It stands as an intrusive focal point for the citizens' attention, a towering, metallic incongruity that disrupts the village's arboreal peace. Worse, though—at least, according to the people of Shale Creek—it serves as a constant reminder of their twenty-four lost months.

By itself, the building on the edge of town might not dispel much of the fog that surrounds Shale Creek's missing time, but it's far from the only discovery the village's citizens made when they found themselves living in their own futures. One of these concomitant discoveries was a profusion of huge ash piles in every homeowner's backyard.

Shale Creek has no waste disposal service, situated as it is in a remote rural locale and populated by only a few hundred families that don't rise to a level of profitability for any waste disposal company's efforts. Instead, residents tend to either compost their trash or burn it in pits and barrels. They are a careful bunch in their fire-starting, though, and rarely allow blazes to roar unattended or without safety barriers. To do otherwise would be to risk disaster, as Shale Creek cannot afford a fire department either. The discovery of numerous large, uncontained ash piles in the backyards of most houses within the village therefore caused a great deal of concern among its residents. These ash heaps denoted massive fires, uncontrolled burns, and careless tending. The people of Shale Creek couldn't believe they would be so irresponsible as to risk the incineration of their homes and the surrounding woodlands. It was so unlike them, so out of character. But the piles suggested otherwise.

What the Shale Creek residents burned is a matter of uncomfortable debate. Raking through the ash in their yard, Sarah and Jamie Linner uncovered several pairs of wire-frame glasses—some remarkably similar to those worn by the Linner sisters themselves. The Booth family sifted from their ash a pair of wedding and engagement rings which appeared to be exact duplicates of the rings worn by Mr. and Mrs. Booth, down to the engravings. Sunlight glinted the same off the gold and silver Celtic cross Jon Dreitzel fished from the ash in his yard as it did off the gold and silver Celtic cross he wore around his own neck.

Katie Fultz found a half-melted retainer in the same neon pink color she wore every day. Bryce Gilman dug up a scorched belt buckle with a screaming eagle on it no different than one he had fastened to his own belt. Jenny Seeder stumbled upon the cracked face of a watch that mirrored the one she wore on her wrist. Other citizens of Shale Creek made comparable discoveries in their yards.

The items found in the ashes prompted Shale Creek residents to whispered speculation. Some claimed the burned items were forgeries that people put to flame in disgust over what must have been a rash of attempted identity theft. Others claimed the burned items were authentic and their currently worn doubles were the forgeries, that someone must have tried to destroy the originals in order to pawn off fakes to the villagers but failed to hide the damning evidence. Children suggested *both* the burned and the worn items might be authentic, but adults dismissed this notion as the influence of too much science fiction and fantasy in their kids' lives.

On the surface, then, the Shale Creek citizens' two explanations for their duplicate discoveries seem rational enough. Most goods—even expensive pieces of jewelry—are produced in mass quantities, and personalizations such as the Booths' wedding ring engravings are easily copied. However, these explanations refuse to address the ash piles themselves. What did the people of Shale Creek burn besides their own personal accessories? If it was possible to reconstitute a thing from its ashes, what would rise from those piles in Shale Creek? No one in the village likes to entertain questions on this matter, as it provides far too much fodder for strange dreams and nightmares, of which the people of Shale Creek already have plenty.

Moving beyond the ash piles, the residents of Shale Creek also discovered a wealth of paraphernalia in their houses and cars relating to something called "the Train." Banners and flags reading "Get on Board THE TRAIN" hung from their front porches. Bumper stickers that proclaimed "THE TRAIN's A-Comin'" clung to the rear fenders of their cars. Buttons with slogans of "Feed the Engine!" and "Get ABOARD or get RUN OVER" were fastened to many of their jackets and scarves and hats. Shirts adorned with phrases like "Next stop: Paradise" and "Choo Choo Chew 'Em Up" lay in laundry baskets across the village. At no point, though, did anyone discover any literature explaining what "the Train" may have been or why it was worth support. Internet searches also proved inconclusive, as "the Train" was a supremely ambiguous phrase and returned hundreds of millions of potential definitions.

Despite a lack of firm evidence, the people of Shale Creek assumed "the Train" had a political connotation. Maybe, they thought, it was a reference to the 2016 election, which they could not remember. But voting records show that not a single person in Shale Creek cast a ballot in November of 2016. If "the Train" dealt with politics, it was only a fraction of a concept that, for the citizens of Shale Creek, must have had far more wide-reaching ramifications.

What, then, did supporting "the Train" entail? As the people of Shale Creek delved further into their missing time, they found numerous disturbing indicators that it may have involved violence. Every member of the Clancy family, for instance, pulled hunting knives from beneath their mattresses, each blade engraved with the word TRAIN on one side and the first name of one of the Clancys—even their three-year-old son and five-year-old daughter—on the opposite. Rich Middleford found a rifle mounted above his bed with the phrase TRAIN CONDUCTOR burned into its stock. Beneath the old oak trees that encircled her house, Nichole Nestor picked up several thick lengths of rope that had been fashioned into nooses, all of which bore frantic marker scrawls on their loops that read "THE TRAIN TO PARADISE." As with the ash piles, other residents stumbled upon other Train-branded implements of destruction in and around their homes.

What use these "Train" weapons served or were supposed to serve, no one knows. Some people insist they're merely ornamental tchotchkes, like posters from a concert or snow-globes from a tourist trap, but the majority of Shale Creek denizens suspect otherwise. If a hunting knife exists in Shale Creek, odds are it skinned an animal; if a rifle hangs in someone's house, it's certainly been shot. The people of Shale Creek are nothing if not practical. But, given this fact, the questions loom even larger. What did those knives dissect? What did that rifle fire upon? What hung from the nooses the citizens of Shale Creek had tied so tight? No one can be certain, though residents of Kellersville, the nearest town to Shale Creek, may provide some answers.

The people of Kellersville and the people of Shale Creek maintain a relationship of mutual dependence. Kellersville is chock full of small retail stores, grocers, and restaurants that only manage to remain open because of the patronage they receive from nearby rural villages like Shale Creek. Likewise, without Kellersville's stores and restaurants, the people of Shale Creek would have no ready access to even the most basic supplies and food services. The two peoples therefore interact on a regular basis. Some might even call them friends. As friends, then, the citizens of Kellersville tell an unusual story about the citizens of Shale Creek.

What the people of Kellersville say is this: beginning in the summer of 2016, people from Shale Creek began to act different. Their way of speaking grew simple, with many smaller words being replaced by grunts and hoots and more complex words disappearing from their vocabulary altogether. When they did string together a few coherent words, they talked of nothing but "the Train" and how great "the Train" was and how "the Train" was going to take everyone to a better place. When the people of Kellersville asked what, exactly, "the Train" was and how it would make life better, Shale Creek residents couldn't articulate answers. They stammered. They stuttered. Their faces flushed. And, ultimately, they responded with a refrain: "the Train is good, the Train is right," their tone gaining force, madness, and rage with every repetition.

The people of Kellersville found it increasingly difficult to converse with their Shale Creek patrons, who had until then been congenial and ready for a quick chat. Before the summer of '16, the people of Shale Creek had never been so quick to anger or so single-minded in their interests. Granted, they were by no means an intellectual or philosophical people, but they had formerly held a sort of pragmatic wisdom that now seemed forsaken. That they became slavish adherents to this "Train" and its inarticulate doctrines made the people of Kellersville uneasy. *How can they be so devoted to nonsense?* the Kellersville residents thought. *Why do they insist on giving up their own voices to this thing?* No one from Shale Creek would—or perhaps could—address these questions, either.

As the summer of 2016 wore into autumn, the residents of Shale Creek gradually severed their ties to Kellersville. They showed up in the town less and less and, on the rare occasion they did visit, they glowered at everyone they saw, openly brandishing knives and guns on their persons as if in threat. If any Kellersville native attempted to engage them in conversation they shoved past that person, sometimes violently, and continued on with their business. Sometimes they'd even utter a vulgarity, draw out their weapons, and shout "Off the track!" It was, some in Kellersville said, as though everyone from Shale Creek had lost their souls overnight.

Then, in early 2017, the people of Kellersville began to notice something impossible and disturbing about the few Shale Creek residents who still dropped into town: when they moved, they became blurry, like long exposure photographs. Their bodies seemed to be in multiple locations at once, as if they'd been stretched out over space-time or were unfolding from themselves. The people of Kellersville assumed this distortion must have been a hallucination due to brain injury or faulty eyesight and ran to neurologists and ophthalmologists for check-ups. But doctors assured them that their brains and eyes were not injured or faulty in the slightest. Something was wrong with the people of Shale Creek, not the people of Kellersville. What that "something" might have been, though, no one in Kellersville understood.

By the middle of 2017, people from Shale Creek no longer visited Kellersville. This development brought much relief to Kellersville's citizens, who preferred to forget what they'd seen, what the people of Shale Creek had become. It was better that way. It let them go about their days without having to worry about what "the Train" really was or the possibility that they, too, might end up like the people of Shale Creek. As far as the people of Kellersville were concerned, Shale Creek had ceased to exist.

But, of course, it hadn't, and a little over a year after they'd vanished, the residents of Shale Creek returned to Kellersville in droves. Their movement no longer blurred, and their bodies seemed fixed in space and time. They talked to storekeepers in full sentences again, making no mention of "the Train," and acted as though nothing in their relationships with the people of Kellersville had been damaged.

The disposition of the residents of Shale Creek had also changed with their reemergence. Gone was the explosive rage, the nonsense sloganeering. Instead, the people of Shale Creek spoke slowly and with little tonal change. They took long pauses between thoughts and paced their speech with heavy sighs. Their shoulders slumped; red, puffy flesh ringed their eyes. Everything in their demeanor conveyed profound depression. When they talked to the people of Kellersville, they made mention only of their confusion, their helplessness. They felt, they said, that they'd lost something entirely irreplaceable. However, they didn't specify that "something" as their unremembered two years. For whatever reason, they seemed to avoid giving the lost "something" any name or further description, which the people of Kellersville thought—and still think—unusual.

Does any of this information resolve the enigma of the ash piles or "the Train?" No. Clearly not. But the experiences of the Kellersville citizens *do* provide further pieces to the puzzle of Shale Creek's missing time. Though these pieces may not fit together neatly, they form a ramshackle frame for the mystery and give a semblance of shape to questions no one has yet asked.

One such question might be: "Couldn't the missing two years be partially filled in by examining the phone and credit records of Shale Creek's citizens?" The answer here is complicated. Phone records show that calls from Shale Creek cellular phones and land lines dropped to near zero for the two shrouded years. The Shale Creek residents made no outgoing calls and only a few close relatives and friends made incoming calls—and even those handful of well-wishers eventually dwindled to nil. However, after friends and relatives stopped calling, an incoming number from an unknown U.S.-based location begins to pop up in every telecom history: 010-101-0045. This number, by all rights, cannot exist. There is no area code 010 in the United

States, thus nowhere for the call to originate, despite what records indicate. Beyond that fact, the number is now disconnected and, when dialed, results in an automated "Not in Service" message. Yet, during the missing two years, Shale Creek residents spent anywhere from two minutes to two hours connected to this defunct line.

Credit records reveal equal strangeness. The people of Shale Creek made no purchases outside of Kellersville during the two-year span—at least, not by debit or credit card. Many of their bills, therefore, went unpaid. Numerous creditors sent collection agents to Shale Creek to prompt payment, but each agent resigned their post in a brief email to their employer after being assigned to Shale Creek and, subsequently, fell off the face of the earth. Thus, the people of Shale Creek continued to accrue untold debt even as no one would—or possibly *could*—collect on it. Without using debit or credit in an age of technology, one wonders how they didn't starve, how their homes and vehicles didn't fall into disrepair. Perhaps they purchased products and services with hoarded physical money. Perhaps they bartered goods for goods and services for services. Or, perhaps, as one Kellersville resident idly suggested, "They were fueled by some kind of irrational hate, and I guess it sustained them in a way nothing else could. They didn't need our food or merchandise anymore because they didn't need anything except 'the Train.' Even as it poisoned them, it was their bread and water."

These records, then, compiled independently and kept with meticulous precision, offer tantalizing crumbs of information, but fail to clarify the situation in Shale Creek during the missing two years. At best, they offer still more frustrating clues, more puzzle pieces that cannot be easily integrated with the rest.

So where does all this leave the mystery of Shale Creek?

Unsolved, as it will likely remain.

The "right" questions are, perhaps, beyond asking. And even if the "right" questions could be posed, it's possible no one would accept their answers. So, Shale Creek remains a forgotten place filled with a people who have forgotten themselves. No amount of third-party information can fill their gaps in memory. No mnemonic devices can clear their fog. Whatever violence they performed during those missing two years, whatever essence they sacrificed to the Train, whatever heaven they were trying to reach, they are now left to fend for themselves. If the Train *did* exist, it took them nowhere even as it collected an unbearable fare. And if the Train never existed at all? Well, in that case, Shale Creek proves that the powers of delusion are stronger than anyone may think—so strong, in fact, that they can erase a people and maybe, just maybe, time itself.

Rules and Regulations of White Pines, Vermont

Written and made available by the White Pines Community Council

Introduction:
You've decided to settle in beautiful White Pines! Wonderful! You're about to become one of the over three-hundred residents of a town that is, without exaggeration, a tiny piece of heaven on earth.

For almost two centuries, White Pines has stood as a testament to a simpler and better way of life. Here in White Pines, we believe in charity, love, and dedication to our neighbors—virtues that have made us a largely self-sufficient and self-sustaining community. If you don't want to travel dozens of miles to a grocery store or your child's school or your demoralizing job, well, don't worry, because you won't have to! We have a foolproof system that will take care of all those headaches and allow you to live as the divine spirit of creation intended!

Given that many of our residents have been raised in the urban and suburban blight to the south, you might be naturally concerned about crime, but in White Pines the crime rate has remained stable at absolute zero for many, many decades. You don't even need to lock your door at night! And if you're worried about your health? Well, the very air in White Pines must be an elixir of life, since, at 99.9 years, the median lifespan of a White Pinesian is over twenty years longer than the national average! We grow 'em good and ripe up here in the mountains! Despite not holding "traditional" jobs (though we think the jobs in our town are actually the most traditional of all), you'll also find White Pines residents are never in want of money, goods, or services. We make sure your needs are met so you can explore what it truly means to be a human BEING rather than a human DOING.

So what, you might have already asked yourself, is the catch? Truly, there isn't one. We've met you, interviewed you, and you've been welcomed to join us! If you can simply adhere to a few basic rules and regulations that all White Pinesians abide by, you'll be set! Trust us, they're easy to understand and even easier to follow. In no time at all, you won't even think of them as rules, but as your natural way of living!

Without further ado, then, here are...

The Rules and Regulations of White Pines:

1. **You must love history and be glad to celebrate it.** White Pines has a long and storied past and we cherish that fact. Especially important to us, and commemorated with a Pioneer Festival each year, is our founding by Henry Ember and Thomas Childs, two scholars from early nineteenth century Boston. Ember, a schoolteacher, and Childs, a minor poet, had been heavily influenced by the Transcendentalist movement sweeping the young nation. Both believed a return to the wilderness would

bring humankind back into alignment with its inherent perfection, and both believed it was their duty to aid in this process. They saw themselves as ministers of a humanist-naturalist faith, gentle heroes who might flush the poisons of the world from the body politic. With the most noble of intentions, Ember and Childs set out, like many other visionaries of their day, to build a sylvan utopia upon the goodness of the human heart. Over the course of several years, they recruited skilled workers to join their community and, in 1839, once their numbers had grown to just over sixty men and women, they trekked northwest in search of a rural idyll in which to plant the seeds of a new Eden. White Pines is the fruit that grew from that labor. We believe it only right to remember and give thanks for such forward thinking and bravery, without which we would not know the paradise that is our town.

2. **You must love nature and seek to conserve it.** Our community is hemmed in on all sides by the breathtaking Green Mountains and our founders intended it to be so. They wanted to inhabit a land so remote that the power and majesty of nature would be unavoidable and all-pervasive. By inundating their senses with the natural world, they hoped to create psychic barriers between White Pines and the corrupt civilization they'd left behind. They were sure that a moss-lined glade was better than a soot-belching factory, that a field of flowers was better than a field of dead soldiers, that the bite from a rattlesnake was better than the bite from a mugger's knife. Turns out, they were right! You'll see that nature is central to our way of life. From our buildings—every last one a log cabin—to our food—all of which is resourced directly from the mountains around us, nature provides for us an unimaginable bounty. In White Pines, we have never experienced drought or flood, famine, or blight. We have

never gone without a meal, nor have we ever wanted for shelter or heat or even a cool breeze on a summer's day. We've remained untouched by diseases and illnesses that decimate other places, other peoples. Nature delivers all this to us and, in return, only asks that we give respect and a bit of sacrifice. It's more than a fair trade-off, we're sure you'll agree.

3. **You must visit Ember's Hole and listen to your name echo in its depths.** There is no feature of the surrounding wilderness so important to our town as Ember's Hole. In fact, Henry Ember and Thomas Childs chose the location of White Pines based solely on its proximity to the hole. From the outset, they recognized the hole's significance as a unique natural feature that could be found nowhere else in New England or, very possibly, the entire world. When you visit the hole, you'll immediately notice exactly what Ember, Childs, and their band of dreamers did—that within fifty paces of the vast depression, sound does not carry. You'll speak but hear nothing; birds above will chirrup and tweet, but their songs will not reach you; even the wind itself cannot whistle in your ear. As you move closer to the hole, you'll become acquainted with its shape and dimensions: a perfect circle with a diameter of nine feet, nine inches. If you hover by the edge of this circle, you'll begin to hear noises from deep within its lightless recesses. The sounds that the surrounding area lacks will seem to you collected, compressed, and distorted far, far below the earth's crust. It is not unusual to hear what you may believe to be pleas or lamentations issue from the hole. Trust that these are mere distortions of the noises of the natural world and no more. From your position on the precipice, then, you will kneel and hang your head over the abyss. Many newcomers stare into the hole and wonder what lies at its terminus. Many feel a sensation they've never felt before, a perfect serenity and

stillness at the center of a cyclone of fear—Henry Ember and Thomas Childs called it the "dread peace." All this is to be expected. No matter what happens to you, whether your experiences at the hole are usual or unusual, you must speak your name into the darkness and wait for it to be repeated to you. Once you hear your voice swirling through the rushes of the harrowing ambience, you will begin to understand what it means to be a part of White Pines.

4. **You must care for your White Pines neighbors and treat them as brothers and sisters.** A rumor you'll hear about town is that Norman Rockwell stumbled upon White Pines as a young man and based many of his illustrations and paintings on scenes he witnessed while in our community. While we can neither confirm nor deny the veracity of that rumor, we can say that the bucolic harmony in many of Rockwell's works is exactly what you'll experience in White Pines. It's rare to see a frowning face about town and it's rarer to hear a heated argument. You'll never be caught up in a drunken brawl—though we do imbibe frequently—and you'll never be cheated out of your fair share of our goods. Some of us claim that even babies don't cry within our borders. There's a humming spirit of togetherness that you can't help but let reverberate inside you. It draws out frustration and anger and sadness and replaces them with a universe of contented smiles. Open yourself to this spirit, this vibrato of perfect community, and we're certain you'll come to love each and every member of the White Pines family.

5. **You must take time to reflect on the joys of living in White Pines and the luck you had in finding us.** We don't ask for reverence or worship, but we do implore you to contemplate the happiness our town will inevitably cultivate within you. Think

on the fact that your pantry is always stocked with fine, organic meats and cheeses and grains and vegetables, even when you don't restock it yourself and that the generator that powers your cabin is always filled with gasoline. Think on the miracle of your children learning to read and write and manipulate numbers without ever listening to a teacher's drone or setting themselves to a page of homework. Think on the impossibility that whatever material goods you request from the town council, they will provide to you regardless of cost. Think on the revelation that your life consists of simply being, that you can choose to sit on your porch and stare at clouds practically all day, every day, and no one will force you to do otherwise. And always remember that exceedingly few people manage to discover our town. You are one of a rarified group selected by happenstance or destiny or the hand of a higher power to stumble upon us. Whether you lost your way from a hiking trail or a camping trip or a Bigfoot hunting expedition, your path through the wilderness led you here—a statistical improbability, considering the acreage of the Green Mountain range. You should have run into a road or a stream and followed its rush back to the corruption of civilization. You should have died from hypothermia, from dehydration, from falling off a rock face or worse. You should have never been able to find us. Yet here you are, in White Pines. Consider that tremendous improbability and know you won a cosmic contest you didn't even have to enter.

6. **You must participate in the lunar drawing and select a named location from your chosen coordinates if you win the drawing.** Twice per month—once on the evening of the full moon and again on the evening of the new moon—we hold a lottery in the center of town. During the lottery, everyone in the community gathers around a hollow wooden globe carved by

one of White Pines' founding members during the mid-nineteenth century. Cut into the north pole of the globe is a hole and from that hole a member of the town council randomly pulls a slip of paper with the name of a White Pines resident written upon it. The globe is then emptied and refilled with new slips of paper. If you're the White Pinesian whose name was selected, you will draw out six of these new pieces of paper—all of which will be inscribed with a letter N, S, E, or W and numerals ranging from zero to one hundred and eighty. These six numbers form latitudinal and longitudinal coordinates that you, the lottery winner, must subsequently plot on a detailed world map held in possession by the town council. You will then list the nine nearest human settlements to the intersection of the coordinates—be they thriving cities or nameless villages—and choose one of these settlements for a special honor. How you select the settlement is entirely at your discretion. Some White Pinesians like to close their eyes and point to one; others simply pick the name that nestles most comfortably in their ears. No matter how you choose, you will eventually close upon one place, one habitation, and inform the town council of your decision, after which you may resume your normal activities and routines and forget all about the lottery as best you can.

7. **You must perform a service for White Pines and be glad to give back to the town.** At random intervals, certain jobs become unavoidable. However, the work we undertake in our community is unlike work in the wider world. At a necessary and proper time, the town council will seek you out and ask for your assistance in dealing with a problem. You cannot refuse to help. Often, the task set before you will be opaque. You might have to walk to a nearby dirt road, find an abandoned car, and drive it to a second location; you might have to venture into the forests and

pick specified berries and mushrooms which you'll be asked to crush into a paste; you might have to carry an unmarked package to a mailbox in a wayward hamlet and make sure it's picked up for delivery; you might have to dig a ditch deep in the forest and sprinkle lye flakes across its bottom. It's impossible to speculate as to what service the council may ultimately need you to perform. Though you may not understand the need for a particular labor, rest assured that each and every action builds toward the maintenance of White Pines and its way of life. It's only through these small gestures of solidarity and allegiance that we manage to remain a safe haven removed from the degradation of civilization and its harmful, ever-extending grasp.

8. **You must let go of the world beyond our borders and distrust its encroachment.** Although we have satellite television and Internet thanks to one of our technologically savvy residents, you'll find we rarely speak of the world outside White Pines. It's not that we don't track its progress or borrow from its advances, but that its general existence threatens ours. When Henry Ember and Thomas Childs shrugged off Boston, they shrugged off the yolk of responsibility to the teeming masses of the city. They understood that not everyone can or should be a member of White Pines. For White Pines to function in its current pristine state, it must remain separate and self-contained. It must remain a space apart. Our peace and prosperity is built upon adherence to our specific rules and regulations, but not all people would respect, let alone follow, those rules. Just imagine if everyone and anyone tried to move here! Our natural splendor would be slashed away, our sense of community would be stretched paper thin, and our traditions would be diluted or supplanted. All the benefits of living in White Pines, all the privileges, all the uniqueness, would crumble. You see then why, for

the sake of our town and your own happiness, you must begin to conceive of the world outside our town as a lost cause. Paradise can ill afford an open-door policy.

9. **You must agree to be lowered into Ember's Hole and etch a name on its walls.** Following lunar drawings, the town council will instruct one member of our community to spelunk into Ember's Hole and etch the name of the lottery winner's chosen settlement into the hole's rock face. Henry Ember was the first to do so and, when it comes your time, you will follow suit. Upon discovering the hole, Ember and Childs experienced what they referred to as "a revelation of the roots of the world in their widest extensions." They wrote that "the hole is where these roots call out for nourishment and where we must supply them such, if they are to bear our community as their brightest and fullest bloom." Thus, we have fertilized those roots twice per month, every month since our founding. Inside the hole, under the tides of rebounding sound, you will find hundreds of names carved into the rock face. Bhopal. Halifax. Aberfan. Dhaka. Benxi. Texas City. Oppau. Some of these names may be familiar to you. Most will be entirely foreign. Ignore them all. You have one reason for entering the hole and one reason alone: to strike a new name into the lightless places. During this process, you'll be suspended by a secure harness inside a cavity that, to the present day, has never been able to be measured to its floor. A crisp odor some have likened to blood will drift into your nostrils and mouth. Your sole source of illumination will be a pocket flashlight. You will be battered by potentially disturbing noises which are often reported to increase in number and volume when you begin etching a new place into the hole. Given these conditions, you will not have the resources—physically or psychologically—to take account of the individual locales listed along the

long, downward spiral. Therefore, it is best to simply chisel the name given to you into an open space upon the wall and signal for your return. After you've been pulled back to the surface and are free of the duty, we're sure you'll agree that spending more time inside Ember's Hole collecting names is the last thing you or any White Pinesian wants to do. Instead, return to your long life of peace and leisure and enjoy the reward that feeding Ember's "roots" affords you.

10. **You must keep the knowledge of White Pines to yourself and help maintain its secrecy.** Since we've established that White Pines requires strict separation from the greater world if it's to bestow its benefits to its members, the next logical step is to safeguard that separation. The wonders of our community are manifold, but they are fragile. Even a single misspoken word to a relative or acquaintance who doesn't live in White Pines could open our town to infection. This means that you cannot invite family to visit; you cannot tell friends where you live; you cannot list White Pines as an address on any document, anywhere. Though we do not require it, we strongly suggest that you rely on your fellow White Pinesians for love and friendship and find the strength to cut yourself off from those who still reside in the outside world. We know this is difficult but doing so will alleviate the temptation to divulge information of White Pines' existence and whereabouts. If at any point in your infrequent travels beyond our borders you do hear non-residents talking about White Pines, you must prevent such persons from continuing their dialogues. Preferred methods of prevention include derision, distraction, and drowning out the speakers. Other, more extreme methods of prevention are available and will be outlined by the town council in an individual meeting with you once you've become a long-term resident. Although occasionally necessary, we suggest utilizing these alternative, more

extreme silencing methods sparingly, as they often draw unwanted attention too near to our community. Perfection, we've found, flowers best in shadow.

11. **You must value tradition and honor its fundamental place in our community's existence.** White Pines stands upon a solid bedrock of stasis. As with any endeavor that accomplishes its goals, we see little reason to promote change when our system of living works better than any other in all the history books in all the world. For nearly two hundred years, we have maintained a quality of life that grants extreme longevity, unparalleled security, and total material prosperity. Our traditions serve as the pillars that prop up and stabilize such a life. Some of these key customs we've outlined in this document—the lottery, the etching of names, and the performance of council tasks for example. Others, like the annual spring warding or the recitation of Thomas Childs' "Ode to the Rift" before town meetings, you will come to know through your basic citizenly participation in White Pines. No matter how you encounter our traditions, you must respect them and understand that they are necessary threads in the protective tapestry that enfolds us. If you tug at one too hard, it may unravel and undermine the integrity of the entire fabric. But if you safeguard each and every fiber, the cloth may last forever.

12. **You must refrain from thinking about the names etched on the walls of Ember's Hole and the jobs you perform for the town council.** Wondering at the meaning of the names and the purpose of the tasks will set you on a path to paranoia and anxiety. While occasional conjecture among other White Pinesians concerning these topics is expected and perhaps even healthy, we insist that exploration into these issues be limited to the

realm of the abstract. A lively philosophical discussion about the power of names or the value of isolation or even the nature of production and scarcity would be encouraged. An investigative project that attempts to specifically link these concepts with Ember's Hole and White Pines' practices, however, while not explicitly prohibited, would be discouraged in the strongest terms. Past instances of community members embarking upon such projects has resulted in expulsion, re-education, and other, less congenial, forms of censure. If your curiosity concerning the basis for our various ceremonies and functions simply cannot be contained, perhaps you will need to turn your inquisitive mind upon yourself. Why do you need to know how words like "Nakhon" and "Pathom" relate to the full set of rare action figures that appear in your cabin when your child asks for them? How does it enrich your life to note that the packages you've been tasked with mailing are, by and large, addressed to journalists? What good can come of recording the cacophony that emanates from Ember's Hole and singling out individual voices that wail for lost children and lovers and parents and friends? How can your life, a life lived in near-total comfort and ease, be made better through any of the knowledge you seek? Answer questions such as these first, before you continue your explorations into the deep state of White Pines. Through your self-examination, we believe that you will realize any true heaven requires a margin of blissful ignorance. Of course, if you fail to reach this conclusion, we hold no liability for your future wellbeing.

13. **You must agree that the perfection of White Pines is sacrosanct and adhere to the rules that safeguard its existence.** Although we cherish each and every member of our community, the overarching project of White Pines is far more important than any individual. Henry Ember and Thomas Childs set out to

expand what it could mean to be a fully realized human being, free from the chains of want, free from the poisons of civilization, and free from the blades of hatred that cut deep in every other corner of the world. White Pines is the attainment of those dreams. Uphold the rules set forth in this document and you'll contribute to a genuine utopia. Disregard or break the rules and, as a cowed Adam and Eve discovered before you, you'll be subject to harsh penalties. We're certain you'll make the right decisions and act as an upstanding citizen of our community. Welcome home.

The White Factory

HI THERE. THE name's James, calling in from... let's just say about as far north as you can go in these United States. The weirdest experience of my life? Well, Chuck, that's an easy one, but I doubt that even you're gonna believe me. I mean, I've been living with this story for twelve years, and I've never dared to tell anyone else about it. Not my ex-wife or my kids. Not one word about the White Factory or what happened there. Most of the time, I try to forget about the whole incident, because, if I'm being really honest, it scares the shit out of me. I don't know, though. Maybe it's the time of night or maybe it's the bottle of Jack in my belly, but I finally wanna get this story off my chest. I think I need to. I need someone to tell me I'm not crazy—or that crazy is pretty much the default for the whole damn world.

Anyway, I'm getting sidetracked. So, weirdest experience, okay. It's summer, twelve years ago, and I'm still a long-haul trucker back then. I'd been jockeying rigs since I turned nineteen, pounding the asphalt from Seattle to Miami and Boston to L.A., just like my grandfather and my father and a bunch of my uncles had before me. I guess diesel runs in my blood. Being out on the road like that is lonely work, though, even for someone who was born into it. Real lonely work. I spend hours staring at taillights, just thinking about how the highway's more my home than the house where my family lives. Hell, I spend more nights in my bunk than my bed. Always makes me real hollow, imagining the road as my home. Like living on a line between two points, neither here nor there. But trucking is the job I've chosen, and it pays well—better than any other minimum wage racket I could've wrangled myself into, anyway—so wherever the load takes me, I'll roll.

At the moment, though, I'm not rolling. I'm standing by my cab, sweating rivers under bright moonlight. Like I said, it's summer. The hot-as-hell part of summer, where after the sun goes down the air hangs completely limp from the beating it's taken all day. I've just made a midnight delivery at a warehouse outside of Cincinnati, and I've been pounding coffee for the past three hours. My hands are shaking a little, and my heart's beating like I just ran a mile uphill, so it's no surprise that when my phone rings unexpectedly, I almost jump out of my skin. Only tragedy calls after midnight, my mother always told me.

I answer and wait for a serious voice to tell me that my wife has been in an accident or that one of my kids has been arrested or maybe both. But it isn't bad news that greets me. It's my dispatcher—a hulk of a guy, like professional wrestler big, with a hard rasp from smoking for thirty years. He whispers over the line, "Hey. You wanna make some serious money tonight?" I'm flying on caffeine. I could drive to China and back. So I say, "Sure," without any consideration.

My dispatcher huffs in satisfaction and goes on. He still isn't talking above a whisper, and he seems hurried, both of which are kinda weird. Anyway, he tells me I gotta deadhead to the pickup, that I'm gonna get five times my usual pay for this load, that I have to be at the pickup location tonight, not tomorrow. He gives me an Ohio address and then, without so much as a thanks or a see ya later, hangs up. Really odd, I thought, because he normally talks my ear off about politics or sports or his kids. But whatever. I don't dwell on it. Nope. My heart's beating too fast, and I'm too busy counting the zeroes on my paycheck. Instead, I just climb in my truck, look up the address on my GPS—this was before our phones could do that—and put the hammer down. My destination sits a little over a hundred and fifty miles to the east, and I want to make it there in less than three hours.

Now, I know you're based down there, Chuck, but if any of you listeners out there have never been to south central Ohio, you might not realize how haunted it feels. As you travel west to east, the land gets wilder, with more hills and fewer valleys, more forest, and less field. The cities thin to towns, and the towns wear away to little villages where half the houses are stripped of paint and missing shingles on their roofs. Eventually even those dying villages fade into the background, so that all you're left with is an occasional boarded-up house or out-of-business gas station. Add in a ton of ancient Native American burial mounds and earthwork sites—like that big-ass snake they got down there—and you've got yourself a place that feels like it's thick with eyes, even if they're staring at you from a distant time. As I roll toward my pickup, I start to creep myself out. It's the middle of the night. I don't pass any other cars or trucks for miles at a stretch. I swear I keep seeing huge red eyes pacing my cab in the darkness alongside the road, but it may be my imagination. Then again, maybe not. One way or the other, I lock my door and put the pedal to the metal.

Well, by two-thirty I'm getting close to the address my dispatcher gave me. Turns out it's situated right on the Ohio River. A lot of factories and power plants and big, nameless, menacing industrial buildings dot the length of the Ohio, and I assume my destination is going to be one of those. I haven't seen a house—abandoned or otherwise—for twenty minutes. The rural roads

I'm driving on are lined by thick spans of forest and wild, overgrown fields. I'm in nowhere country for sure, but I know I gotta be close to the end of the line.

As I keep driving, a nine- or ten-foot-high fence topped with a couple rows of electrified wire pops up at the edge of the woods on my right side. Not exactly a welcome mat. A couple hundred yards down the road, I come to a driveway made of what looks to me like pure white marble and a gate set into the fence line. My GPS finally tells me I've arrived, that this is the place.

I pull into the factory's entrance and feel a little guilty. I can barely believe someone would use marble as a road surface, let alone imagine how much it would cost to install something like that. It seems somehow wrong to drive on it, like I'm committing some kind of sin. I inch up to the gate and roll down my window. Embedded in the driveway just outside the gate is a metal pole with a speaker box mounted to its top.

"Hello?" I shout into the box, over the grumble of my truck's engine. "I'm here to pick up a shipment. I'm from Pleasant Brothers Trucking."

I wait. Nothing happens. I start to worry.

Then, from the speaker, comes a robotic voice. "Proceed forward to the loading bays on the left," it says. Sounds like an answering machine from the 1980s, like it's a prerecorded message on a really cheap cassette tape, with a lot of hiss and fuzz in the background.

The gate retracts, and I pull in. At first, the only thing I see is the white driveway and more forest. No loading bays or a building of any kind. But then the trees thin, and the White Factory comes into view. Imagine a sugar cube sitting on a table. Now place four smaller sugar cubes up against its sides. That's the White Factory. It doesn't have windows or external lights or smokestacks or any fancy logo plastered on it. It's just white.

Really white. Under the glare of my headlights, it's so bright it's almost painful to look at. I wonder if it's made from the same pure marble as the driveway but shoo the idea away. No one in their right mind would build something like that.

The driveway forks into three branches just before it reaches the Factory, and I veer left, as instructed. I see a single trailer backed up against the side of the Factory, so I drive over and start to hitch up to it. I climb down from my cab to ready the fifth wheel, and two things happen at the same time. First, all my coffee from the night starts tearing up my gut and begging to be let out in the nearest restroom. Second, a man with a flashlight held loose at his side strolls up behind me and asks, "Are you here to transport the order?"

I didn't see the guy coming. Didn't hear footsteps, didn't see a door open in the Factory. So I jump a mile in the air and spin around with my fists up like I'm gonna fight someone. But this guy, he just stands there smiling wide, completely relaxed, like he couldn't care less if I take a swing at him. He's the palest person I've ever seen in real life. His skin's the color of a sheet of paper. And he's wearing aviator sunglasses. At almost three in the morning, he's wearing sunglasses.

Well, I lower my fists and huff back, "Yeah, I'm here to pick up."

He keeps smiling—so wide it almost looks painful—and says, "The order will be loaded onto the trailer shortly. Please wait."

He turns off his flashlight and starts to stroll away, but, by now, my need for a restroom has become an emergency. Being scared right out of my boots didn't help one bit. So I run after the guy.

"Do you have a toilet I can use?" I call out. "I've been on the road a long time tonight."

He stops and turns—still has that same damn smile on his face—and says, "Follow me."

He leads me right up to the side of one of the smaller jutting cube parts of the Factory where a little rectangle of the outer wall slides away. If you didn't know a sliding door had been there, you never would've seen it. It's so seamless, almost like the building is covered in a layer of skin that splits open right at that doorway. The pale guy steps through the opening and I hurry after him.

Inside, we walk through a narrow hallway that's really dimly lit. It seems much brighter than it is, though, because everything—the floors, the ceiling, the walls—are all made of the same crazy white stone as the exterior of the Factory and the driveway. Again, I don't see any windows or doors—just blank white space without any personality. I kinda wonder how anyone could stand working here. I think it'd drive me insane.

The guy, who, in the light, I can now see is wearing a black suit with a black tie and black undershirt, stops at a random spot in the hallway and motions to one of the walls. Again, part of the seemingly solid white surface slides away to reveal a room.

"Relieve yourself and then please exit the facility by the same path you used to enter," the pale guy says, sort of bored, sort of, I don't know, hollow.

I duck inside the room that just opened up and, what do you know, it's a restroom—all white and shiny like the rest of the place. The stone wall snaps shut behind me and I worry for a second that I'm trapped. Not that it matters though, because, at the moment, I have more pressing matters to attend to.

I take care of business and, after I'm finished, I walk up to the wall, and it automatically slides open for me. The hall beyond it is deserted. I don't see the pale guy anywhere. But I do hear something, something that sends my stomach turning again: the voices of what has to be about a billion people screaming and moaning and screeching. It's a muffled noise, sort of distant, but I can definitely hear it.

Now, I know I shouldn't be curious. I know I should just block out this strangeness and go to my truck. But I don't. Instead, I track the sound—which tears through me like a breeze from a window open onto hell—all the way to the end of the hall opposite where I came in. I press on the wall at that far end, but it doesn't open for me the way it did for the pale man. Not knowing what else to do, I put my ear against the wall and try pick out any specific words among the screams. I want to understand what's happening, but there's no understanding to be had here—just a billion voices wailing in madness.

I pound on the wall and stomp the floor as hard as I can and yell, "Hello? Do you need help?" over and over. If anyone hears me, they don't answer.

By this point, I'm getting pretty freaked out, so I decide to go to my truck and call someone. Who, I don't know. But I figure someone has to have answers.

The hallway peels open to let me exit, and I walk back to my cab in a hurry. As I near it, I see a gap in the Factory right behind the trailer, a loading dock that hadn't been there before. On the dock, two pale guys dressed in the same all-black suits as the original pale guy are carrying an enormous, mirrored cube toward the open trailer.

"Hey!" I say to them, waving my arms to get their attention, "I think someone's hurt inside your factory. I think they need help. I heard screams."

These guys, they look up as I draw close, the cube losing its balance between them. I stop right beneath the dock, ready to ask for help again, but the thought disappears when the cube topples out of their hands and shatters against the floor.

Several dozen oval things—what I think must be footballs—roll out of the broken cube. A couple reach the end of the dock, where I'm standing, and fall off the edge, into the driveway. I bend to pick them up and give them to the guys on the dock but freeze when I see what they are: heads. Human heads. And they're alive. They're grinning and blinking, and one is silently mouthing swear words and another is making kissy faces at me. I think "robots." I think "zombies." I think "impossible." And now it's my turn to scream. I stumble backward and land on my butt, still watching the heads, which all turn their gazes in my direction.

The guys on the dock jump down to my level and start moving toward me with purpose. I shift my focus away from the heads and start apologizing to the dockworkers, mumbling, "Oh shit, sorry. Sorry. Sorry, guys," but I don't think apology is what these dudes want. I try to meet their eyes to gauge how much anger's coming my way, but I realize I can't because they don't have any eyes. Where their eyes should be is just a patch of smooth, grubworm pale skin.

These eyeless guys in their black suits, they're smiling, real wide, too wide, just like the pale guy in the aviators did, and they're bearing down on me in a hurry. A sick feeling boils up in my stomach. I gotta get out of here. Whatever this place is, it's not right. It's not safe.

Somehow, I manage to roll over and scramble to my feet before the eyeless guys reach me. I run like my life depends on it. I jump into my cab, lock the door, and haul ass away from that Factory faster than lightning, ditching the trailer and the load and, probably, my job. I don't think my speedometer dips below eighty for a couple hours, which is fine by me.

The next morning, when I finally slow down and pull into a truck stop for some rest, I call my company and ask to talk to my dispatcher, expecting to be canned. The receptionist tells me he didn't come in, though. Turns out, he doesn't come in the next day either. Or the next. Or any other day after that. Far as I know, no one ever sees him or hears from him again after that night.

As for me, well, I never trust a load again. I get the sweats and the shakes real bad any time I have to pick up. I can't concentrate on the road in front of me because I'm so worried about what I'm dragging behind me. I can't shrug off those heads in the mirrored box and that White Factory with its pale, eyeless workers. So, about a year later, I quit trucking altogether—a move that I didn't regret then and don't regret now, either.

And that's it. That's the weirdest experience of my life. Maybe someone out there knows how to make sense of it or what it means. I know I can't. All I can say is that if you drive down enough lonely roads, you're going to come to some really strange places. I learned that all too well.

To the Ravine

Though the night can neither conceal our futures nor hide us from ourselves, our task feels less sinful under the blind eye of the moon. I steal a glance behind me, at the girls who hold the lanterns, at the boys who carry the burden on their shoulders. Their visages betray none of the horror to come. Perhaps it's perverse, and perhaps they know it's perverse, but their clear gray eyes sparkle with a hope that I've never seen before.

I climb the trail ahead of them, searching for the right spot, the place where the body will never be discovered, the place where, somehow, the body will always be discovered. I scout nothing but trees and shrubs, trees, and shrubs.

The train of my children catches up to me. The boys lower the cot gently, carefully, as though the bearers of a great king. I turn to them and kick out at the thing on the cot, the thing they have marshaled through the forest. It slides to the side, away from my foot. It knows my every action before my action. It knows my thoughts before I've had opportunity to form them.

I motion for the boys to step back, and I lean down next to the lumpen thing on the cot, the amorphous blob of flesh that is their sibling, my firstborn, our terror.

"Do you know what we're going to do out here?" I ask it.

The thing's single, iris-less eye opens and regards me as it always does—with a chilling clarity borne from absolute indifference.

“Of course,” it intones, in that devastating, flat voice which seems to echo in all directions of space and time. “I die tonight, eventually.”

My children shrink back at this revelation, though they are already so small and so battered from the weight of the thing’s many revelations past.

“Yes,” I say, “yes. You die tonight. And you don’t intend to stop us?”

The thing looks through me. I refuse to know what it sees.

“I do not stop you. You hurl my body into ravine just ahead. You all feel relief. Henry cries, but only because he has never seen a person die. He will never knowingly kill another animal for the rest of his life. On the way back to town, Joanna falls on a rock which imbeds itself in her palm. The wound is not treated properly for hours, and so it scars. She often covers it with gloves because it reminds her of the night when her father murdered her brother. She will concentrate on it during the birth of her first child, who will succumb to influenza in its sixth month of life.”

“Enough,” I bellow, raising my hand in an impotent threat against the thing's grubby body. “This is why we have to be done with you. Because our lives aren’t lives any more. They’re... they’re... parts in a stage play that we’re all acting out. You feed us the lines, and you feed us the directions, and then when we get there, to that scene, we can’t live. We can only... we can only *pretend* that we’re living.”

The thing blinks and looks up at the puzzle of stars above us. It can probably see all the connections between them.

“There is no difference,” it says. “We do what we have done and will do.”

I kick up a clod of soil and leaves. Tarry specks of dirt spatter my child’s hairless head.

"There *is* a difference," I say. "We don't want to know. Why do you think your mother slit her wrists? Because you told her she would. Every day for eighteen years she waited in anxiety, waited for the day to come, her mind never settling, always on an edge. It was the waiting, the knowing, that destroyed her. You planted that seed, and it grew shadows inside her."

The thing turns its attention back to me.

"You have the seed inside you, too," it says. "You are hanging. Men with shining stars dancing on their chests smile. You are turning purple. Your tongue lolls out of your head. Your legs kick at the air. The men laugh. You are dead."

One of my boys, Thomas, steps up behind the thing and slaps the back of its head.

"No," I hold up a hand. "It's told me this before. I know all about this."

My firstborn, that thing which made the doctor shudder and run from our house when it entered the world, closes its eye, and speaks to us all, louder now.

"Father, you are hanging. I am burst in the ravine. Thomas is riddled with bullets. Henry's heart is stopped, as are Billy's and Lucy's. Zachary is crushed beneath a fallen horse. Joanna is suffocated by the fluid in her lungs. We are dead, father. We are all dead. But only I can see it."

"So close your goddamned eye," I scream into the night. My voice withers against the woods and the pinpricked sky. It refuses to travel as far as my child's.

The boys and girls flinch away, seeking shelter from a desperation they know too well. Our every hour has been long revealed to us and the knowledge wears on them as it wears on me.

"I do not," the thing says. "I cannot. It is who I am. It is what I am. I tell you what I tell you. I know what I know."

I laugh at the thing. I laugh at my children. I laugh at the entire universe. And my laughter causes the boys and girls to fidget ever more.

"Then you're the devil," I gasp, "just like Reverend Samuels claimed you were. You come bearing knowledge we don't want. And it's my duty to throw you back down into the pit."

I motion for the boys to pick up their sibling's cot. Without hesitation, they move in.

"If I am your devil," the thing says as it's hoisted into the air again, "then I wonder what you worship."

I reach up and place a hand on the thing's neck, drawing its malformed face to mine.

I want to whisper something profound; I want to throw the thing's perception of the world into as much confusion as it has thrown mine, but no thoughts were ever meant to trickle onto my tongue.

Unable to explain myself and my fury, I spit into the thing's face and rise.

I pump a fist in the air and gather my children.

"Let's find that ravine," I shout. And we march further into the night.

PREFACE TO MITCHELL D. GATZ'S *REVELATION OF THE UNPETTING HAND: THE APOCALYPTIC VISIONS OF DOMESTICATED CANIDAE*

When Dr. Lyra Sciavalli discovered the neural uplink frequency for domesticated dogs fifty-nine years ago, she couldn't possibly have known she was about to open a Pandora's Box that we've yet to close. Certainly, her motivations were pure. Following the same techniques that allowed Dr. Yu Matsuzaka to tap the human brain only four years previously, Sciavalli hoped that attaining a telepathic connection to our faithful canine companions would strengthen our bonds and usher in a deeper understanding between human and non-human spheres of being. It was a utopian dream fashioned after Matsuzaka's own idealistic notion that through a literal meeting of minds, divergent peoples might finally understand the common "humanness" that binds us all and gain a deeper appreciation of foreign cultures, races, religions, and creeds. But, of course, like Matsuzaka's project, Sciavalli's discovery failed to usher in an era of peace and understanding.

In Matsuzaka's case, people simply found new and better fodder for their hatreds; with minds laid bare, it was now possible to discriminate on the basis of thought processes and emotional constitutions. Thus, we saw the rise of hate groups that railed against individuals with thought patterns that shirk conventional logic (e.g., The Rationalist Front), hate groups that targeted those individuals whose mental processes are markedly faster than average (e.g., Deliberationist United), and hate groups that discriminated against individuals who, by the standards of those groups, didn't feel a range of emotion that is "normal" or broad enough (e.g., Soldiers for Sympathy). But even worse than the newly minted hatreds that spawned from telepathic communication was the fact that Matsuzaka's technique allowed us to peer within the dark recesses of one another's thoughts. Suddenly, the heavily guarded doors to all our secret sins and unthinkable desires were thrown wide open. After Matsuzaka, we could no longer look strangers in the eye or trust even our dearest beloved, as penetrating light was suddenly shined upon all those hideous objects that otherwise cast only shadows in the human heart. Thus, of course, the eventual global ban on all Matsuzaka devices.

Into this miasma stepped Lyra Sciavalli, then a young veterinary neurologist who wrote in the *Journal of Exploratory Sciences* that "I anticipate interspecies telepathy will be less fraught with potential ethical dilemmas and hidden ramifications than human telepathy, which, from the very beginning, has seemed an even more perilous undertaking than interstellar travel." (31.2, 194). Following two tedious years of calibration to allow a stable reciprocation protocol between canine and human alpha and beta brainwave frequencies (a fifth of the time it took Matsuzaka to accomplish the same with humans), Sciavalli achieved a successful link with her own companion animal, a seven-year-old male purebred chihuahua named Thunder. In spite of their familiarity, however, nothing could have prepared Sciavalli for what she encountered during the uplink. As she explains in her *Alien Perceptions: The Inner Life of Dogs*, "That first meeting between my mind and Thunder's mind was beyond the bounds of my experience. With people, you understand the symbols and images that flow into you; you have a reference point for basic logic and self-awareness. But with Thunder, it was as if I'd stumbled into a movie theater in another galaxy. I saw visions of objects that I knew, but they were combined with odors and sounds in strange ways, and none of them seemed to hold the same meaning for Thunder as they did for me. There was definitely a rationale to the entire stream of consciousness, but it was rationale I couldn't decipher" (Sciavalli 49).

Sciavalli wasn't deterred by the foreignness of Thunder's thought patterns. She expanded her research, linking to dozens of dogs from various backgrounds and breeds. Over the course of several months, with the aid of a team of psychologists, animal behavioralists, and semioticians, she managed to piece together a canine "language" from which she could interpret basic thoughts such as "I'm bored," "I'm hungry," and "I love you." (Boredom generally represented as a dark, odorless rock that pulses like a heartbeat; hunger represented as a buzzing, glittering maelstrom of blood, flesh, or teeth; and love represented almost universally among canine breeds as a wet tongue curled around a warm light that emanates an odor akin to sweat.)

The linguistic breakthrough gave Sciavalli enough hope to push deeper into the canine psyche. She began to focus on theta wave interaction in an effort to, as she said, "determine whether dogs evince any meaningful subconscious creativity or more complex symbolic thought" (Sciavalli 122). Although she was aware that theta waves are carriers of nightmares and deep-seated fears and was warned by none other than Yu Matsuzaka to "tread lightly in the theta band, for in those waves swim monsters," Sciavalli forged ahead with her experiments (Matsuzaka 217). The results of these theta wave experiments remain, nearly sixty years later, a topic of serious debate and anxious speculation, as what Sciavalli found embedded deep within the canine subconscious was nothing less than profound evidence of precognition.

Just as in conscious canine thought, the subconscious canine mind recombines sensory data into abstruse forms and patterns partially familiar to human systems of symbol but divergent in meaning by several significant degrees. This Sciavalli quickly realized. In her personal journals, she notes that "Thunder's subconscious seems to operate in a manner analogous to my own, hashing and rehashing stimuli from his daily experiences, albeit in unusual configurations" (Journals 303). More importantly, however, Sciavalli also quickly realized that dark incongruities abounded within the subconscious thoughtforms of the dogs with which she'd linked. "Bizarrely, as I sifted through the detritus of these dogs' experiences," she writes, "I repeatedly encountered hazy, nightmarish images of dark, shuffling trees and heartrending sounds of human moans and sobs. One dog in particular, a six-year-old pug named Dixie, presented with these particular thoughts and an additional odiferous sensation of ham and cheese. This addition I found particularly inexplicable and, frankly, disturbing. There was no connection I could make between the smell of ham and cheese and the nightmarish sense of pain, confusion, and loss that Dixie experienced. It didn't make sense" (Journals 334).

Though Sciavalli had seemingly run into a wall, time showed her a path to circumvention. Several months after her link to Dixie, her research team ran follow-ups with every test subject dog and his or her caregivers. In the case of Dixie, it so happened that the pug's caregiver, an elderly gentleman referred to as "Mr. P," had passed away in the intervening months and that Dixie was now a companion for Mr. P's youngest daughter. During the follow-up, Mr. P's daughter made casual mention that "her father had loved Dixie more than anything else in the world, except for maybe ham and cheese sandwiches, which he hadn't eaten in more than fifteen years due to high blood pressure but were served in his honor at his wake" (Journals 336). At first, Sciavalli assumed that Dixie had simply smelled ham and cheese sandwiches that her caregiver had surreptitiously eaten against medical advice. Upon inquiry, though, Mr. P's children and grandchildren all swore that they'd never seen a single slice of ham or a block of cheese anywhere in the old man's home. Even if they had, Sciavalli reasoned, it wouldn't have explained why Dixie felt terror and dislocation in connection with those items.

In a paper published in the futurist journal *Speculative Frontiers*, one of Sciavalli's research assistants, Priya Anusha, became the first to consider that perhaps "Dixie could very well be tapping into a sensory experience – whether conscious or subconscious – that is inaccessible to the human sensorium. Given what recent theories in physics have suggested, it is not outside the bounds of reason and rationale to consider that Dixie may have sensed time in a less linear fashion and, therefore, received precognitive sensations" (Anusha 41). Sciavalli took Anusha's theory quite seriously. As she established deeper links with individual dogs and began to unearth ever more primeval strata of the canine subconscious, she encountered increasingly inexplicable imagery and sensations. "Beneath my encounters with the usual foodstuff-laden sensations of dreams and the common predation sensations of nightmares," she wrote, "I find there are layers of subconscious canine thought that share in no immediate real-world cognate. I'm witness to flaming fields of glass and shadow whips that lash at my back, unearthly moans from no obvious source and saurian roars from insects of monstrous size. The level of abstraction that these thoughts evince is astonishing, but abstraction of *what* I cannot even begin to guess in most instances" (Journals 295).

Sciavalli, at a loss to quantify the deep theta wave sensations as memories, bizarre and unsettling as they were, began a process of cataloguing their intricacies for future analysis. To the best of her ability, she described and recorded each snippet of subconscious experience that she couldn't place within relative approximation to a known canine thoughtform or communicative symbol. Two other members of her research team, the aforementioned Priya Anusha and a graduate student named Oliver Davids, also linked to numerous dogs during theta wave production and added their own entries to the catalogue. In this way, Sciavalli and her associates gradually compiled a compendium of surreal, nigh apocalyptic vignettes – a book that would eventually become *The Unpetting Hand.*

Months after Sciavalli began the cataloguing project (and in some cases even years later), she engaged in a series of follow-up interviews with the caregivers of every dog with which she and her team had linked. During these interviews, she compared her descriptions to the events of the dogs' subsequent lives. Her resultant data revealed that significant, if not overriding, aspects of the thoughts she'd recorded could be explained as metaphorized versions of major events that had occurred within the dogs' lives after the link. As she details in her *Alien Perceptions*:

"In one of my entries I'd written that I'd heard a crashing, tympanic chime repeatedly striking twice in quick succession. This sound was accompanied by a rubbery odor and a feeling of what I could only describe as manic yearning. The visualization that accompanied the thought expressed the same mania, as commonplace objects and places quavered and quaked rapidly before my mind's eye, as though about to explode with internal energy. In a subsequent follow-up with the caregivers of the dog from whom these sensations had arisen, I was told that they had recently lost one of their companion animals to a late-night traffic accident. The animal in question – a Persian cat – had slipped a loose screen door and run onto a nearby road, where it was fatally struck by a motorist. The motorist stopped, rang the family's doorbell twice in rapid succession, and let them know what had happened. The dog with which I'd been linked had a close relationship with the deceased cat; they were inseparable, claimed the caregivers, and the dog so distraught by the Persian's disappearance that he ran about the house without food or sleep for three consecutive days. Here was the doubled ringing, the rubber smell (of tires squealing to a halt), and the manic yearning to find someone or something. The similarities could not be coincidence. These were not entirely abstract symbols. This dog had experienced the future" (Sciavalli 360).

Time and again, details from Sciavalli, Anusha, and Davids' catalogue mirrored subsequent life events of the dogs with which they'd linked. The trio became convinced that the canine thoughts they'd received through the theta wave band were empirically verifiable instances of precognition. Today, their data is still the subject of much scrutiny and debate in psychological, technological, biological, and physics circles (as the existence or non-existence of precognition greatly impacts them all). Many serious scholars and researchers have argued Sciavalli deserves a posthumous Nobel Prize for her work, as theta wave telepathy between human and canine continues to be repeated in labs across the world with the same results –

namely, disturbing, surreal canid visions that, upon follow-up evaluation, are easily equated to traumas and impactful subsequent experiences in those animals' lives. The bulk of the scientific establishment, however, roundly fearing a seismic upheaval of its foundational orthodoxies and thus a collapse of its credibility (and, ultimately, the cultural cache from which it derives its power), refuses to accept these results and remains stalwart in its skepticism, claiming that the visions are "so metaphoric and abstract that they could relate to any experience from the dogs' existence, past or future" (Headley 55).

The scientific credulity of Sciavalli's conclusions is not our concern here, though. Instead, we in the province of canid eschatology are concerned with the entries in *The Unpetting Hand* for which Sciavalli and her team could not find experiential parallels. The field of canid eschatology stemmed from the idea that, if Sciavalli's theories hold weight and her linked dogs did, in fact, access future events, then, perhaps, the recorded thoughts and sensations that cannot be readily attributed to a particular dog's already-lived experience may not necessarily lie in that dog's future lifespan, but in the future of the world writ large. Dr. Marco Trujillo, a sociology and religious studies professor with degrees from several Ivy League schools, was the first to propose that Sciavalli's dogs had acted as conduits for prophecy. In his *Collared Apocalypse*, he remarks that, "The thoughts that are recorded in *The Unpetting Hand* strike me as nothing short of prophetic revelation. In these thoughts, as in most of the major oracular tomes produced throughout history, we find epic scenes of destruction and violence that seem pointed toward an apocalyptic endgame. If for no other reason than to learn more about canine 'culture,' a study of these thoughts as eschatology visions should be taken seriously, though it may be the case that these visions are, as some have claimed, glimpses of our own future filtered to us through unlikely sources – canidoracles, if you will" (Trujillo 396). Thus it was that scholars began to unpack and examine the multitude of entirely unexplained images and sensations from *The Unpetting Hand*, a development that, in effect, allowed canid eschatology to take root in the margins of academia.

As alluded to above, the study of canid eschatology has at its base the most vague and inexplicable entries from Sciavalli, Anusha, and Davids' *The Unpetting Hand*. Such entries are plentiful and, even when compared to the traumatic thoughts and sensations that Sciavalli managed to connect with reasonable real-world cognates, wholly unsettling. Consider the amalgam of images and sensations that has been termed "Winston's Deluge."

In this thought, a good-natured male pug by the name of Winston transmitted to Oliver Davids a series of images of a mega-tsunami crashing down upon a sleek, modern cityscape. In and of itself, this might not be particularly notable. Massive tsunami waves do occur, and it's possible that Winston could have seen a representation of one at some point in his life. However, Winston's Deluge is no ordinary natural disaster, as its destroyer wave isn't composed of water. Rather, the tsunami is a cascade of disembodied human smiles replete with gleaming white teeth and thick, moist lips. As the wave sweeps over the nameless city, the smiles grow wider, longer, godlike, until even a single joyful maw is capable of opening wide and swallowing skyscrapers whole. And this is precisely what the smiles do as they wash over the metropolis – they devour every remnant of human civilization in their path. They sweep through the city and consume business towers, hospitals, grade schools, fast food restaurants, bridges, tunnels, trains, planes, buses, cars, bicycles, fences, mailboxes, sidewalks, portable toilets, and fire hydrants. They inhale it all, and after the wave passes, nothing of the city remains but miles of freshly unearthed topsoil.

The imagery of Winston's Deluge alone would be sufficient to classify it as an eschatological vision, but the complete thought also included "a hollow, giggling sound like the prerecorded laughter of a child's baby doll" and "the undeniable feeling that the body of whomever – or whatever – was witnessing the deluge was about to undergo a radical, possibly painful, transformation to another form that lurked just beneath the original body's surface" (*Unpetting Hand* 188). When combined, these sensations are difficult, if not impossible, to qualify as conventional experience. Even when one evaluates the metaphors as symbolically equitable to metaphors used in human vernacular (e.g., the smiles denoting overwhelming joy, the hollow laughter denoting false happiness), the entire thought remains wholly focused on scorched-earth destruction and presumptive ontological change – both hallmarks of apocalyptic narrative.

Winston's Deluge, however, while certainly interesting in its own right, is not the most complex or disconcerting eschatological vision of Sciavalli's dogs. This honor belongs to the titular Unpetting Hand. Variations of the Unpetting Hand are scattered throughout Sciavalli's team's records and, although permutations of the thoughtform are generally unique from individual dog to individual dog, the basic conception of the Unpetting Hand recurs across nearly the entire canid population with which Sciavalli's team linked.

The vision of the Unpetting Hand tends to begin as a pleasant stroking sensation behind the ears or along the spine. Oftentimes, its percipient sees a glowing hand – variable in size, shape, and skin pigmentation – repeatedly hovering and descending in tandem with the strokes. Sciavalli described the effect as "UFO-like in its utterly silent, eerily unknowable presence" while Davids recorded it as "an all-seeing, all-touching will-o'-the-wisp" and Anusha remarked upon its "celestial, awe inspiring, hand of god" qualities (*Unpetting Hand* 302-310). If this glowing hand occurs as part of the vision, it appears as the sole object within a void. Beyond the hand and its witness, nothing else exists. The mysterious hand and the unseen body, the petter and the petted – these are the only two subjects in all creation.

As the vision draws onward, the stroking sensation gains a hypnotic or sedative quality that marks a turning point, for while the pleasure of the caress rises toward ecstasy, a deep paranoia begins to shadow its growth. At this point, the gaze of the petted percipient slides away from the glowing hand and focuses upon the void. It waits and watches, eyes darting to and fro, paranoia sharpening to anxiety and anxiety sinking into terror. Yet nothing appears in the void. The stroking continues, bodily pleasure increases, terror claws behind the eyes, and still the void remains fixed, silent, and unmoving. Until, that is, the outline forms.

Near the moment when the experience crests the pinnacle of pleasure and terror, *something* begins to take shape within the void. Sciavalli, Anusha, and Davids were all clear in their records concerning this form: it could only be referred to as "something." Sciavalli commented that "To describe it as anything in particular would be disingenuous. It is *something*. *The* something. It is non-specificity made specific. It thwarts rational perception and concrete description. There's no way to sort this thing into taxonomies of experience or being because it's their opposite. It's the as-yet-unexperienced. It's becoming. It's... something" (*Unpetting Hand* 341). Anusha said of her experience of the "something" that "At best I'd call it an even darker outline marked upon what was already absolute darkness, but that doesn't really convey the feeling of the thing or explain its shape, which is both present and yet not present. It sounds mad, but I believe it was the soul of the universe. I believe it was all that is hidden from our feeble anthropoid perceptions" (*Unpetting Hand* 361). Davids writes along similar lines, remarking that:

"It's not a thing. It's the idea of a thing. And what that thing is – well, I felt it, and I couldn't tell you. It was like this: imagine you see a person walking down the street, only they're laterally bisected, they're half a person, split right down the middle. But they're ambling along and laughing and talking and as if the other half was right there, right with them, step for step, and it drives you insane to know where that other half might be and what it looks like and what it's doing and why it isn't there in the first place. It drives you insane to imagine all the possibilities. You're frightened out of your mind because how can this be? Where is the other half? But you're also awe-stricken by the sheer weight of the event and all that it might entail" (*Unpetting Hand* 369).

In one of her later entries, Sciavalli attempts to further elucidate upon the experience and, in the process, coins the most famous lines of the text, lines that function as the fulcrum for much of the study of canid eschatology. Those lines are, of course, the oft quoted: "A fearful thing, a bold new thing, a thing reaching out in love, a thing poised to strike a deadly blow: this is all contained in the future at once. This is all part of what's forever missing from the scene: the other hand. The unpetting hand. The thing that must be somewhere but isn't. The thing that we can imagine, but never, ever know. While one hand pets, what does the other hand do?" (*Unpetting Hand*

399). Sciavalli was never able to answer this question, dying quite tragically and under unusual circumstances at the age of forty-two only a few months after posing it in her records (see D.V. Hernandez's book *A Conspiracy of Muzzles: The Death of Lyra Sciavalli* for an in-depth discussion of her final days). Even in Sciavalli's final hours, however, we can assume that the question haunted her, as within the crushed car where she died was a sea of notebook paper all bearing the same hastily scrawled and repeated phrase: "THE UNPETTING HAND."

With Sciavalli gone, her canine telepathy project lost its funding despite its obvious successes, and her protégés branched out into other arenas of experimentation and study (at the behest of external forces, some claim). Her results, for all their potential import, became the subject of religious fear-mongering and scientific ridicule. Just as spiritual leaders from the monotheistic faiths cried that "Future knowledge is the word of God, and the word of God can only be spoken to his highest creation: humankind," so, too, did scientists from practically every field lambast Sciavalli's work, saying that "It's preposterous to assume that the thoughts of dogs are anything more than the primal recombinative stirrings of lower functioning minds" (Jameson 41, Hertz 17). Without Sciavalli's steady hand to write refutations to such criticism, her work fell out of favor with the mainstream, and the extrapolation and interpretation of her data descended to fringe scholars, scholars who believed Winston's Deluge, the Unpetting Hand, and many other visions were, as Sciavalli and her team increasingly believed, highly metaphorized versions of future apocalyptic events.

It is precisely this study which we undertake in canid eschatology today, as we are those "fringe" scholars. Through the use of literary theory, philosophy, religious studies, and history, we endeavor to make sense of Sciavalli's dogs' theta-wave enlaced thoughts and to discern the potential future scenarios (apocalyptic or otherwise) they may represent. We analyze *The Unpetting Hand* as a text no different than the *Book of Daniel*, the *Revelation of St. John*, or portions of the *Bhagavad Gita*. We try to answer Sciavalli's eternal question and understand what "unpetting hands" may lurk in the darkness of our own world and the minds of humankind's best friends. We pore over the experiences set down in *The Unpetting Hand*, and we consider, to the best of our abilities, the fate of our world that Sciavalli's dogs may have seen stretched out before us.

Of course, the conclusions we often reach in our study of canid eschatology are far from comforting. Detroit University eschatologist Azim Al-Hikmet, for instance, has advocated for a position that sees the Unpetting Hand as "... the flip side of divine love and universal beneficence. If God is capable of eternal kindness, God must also be capable of eternal hatred. If one hand doles out pleasure and riches, without view to consequence, then surely another unseen hand must be waiting to dole out pain and hardship. What the Unpetting Hand shows us is that even in its moments of grace, the divine, the universal, is always preparing to strike us down" (Al-Hikmet 10). Katrina Chaisson, eschatologist at the University of West Central Florida, has reasoned that "the Unpetting Hand is not a representation or a symbolic object; it is a tangible, destructive cosmic force that has been altered by the prism of canine perception, possibly a comet or asteroid. While dogs have no concept of comets or asteroids as celestial bodies, no concept of world-ending impact events, they do, however, have a concept of pain that comes from above, of violence descending upon them, and this is what they see: the Unpetting Hand, a cosmic body(part), our end, floating in space, waiting to throw down its fury upon the furred backside of the earth and extinguish all life" (Chaisson 22). And K.L. Dramford, an independent scholar, has argued, evoking Illuminati conspiracy theory, that "the Unpetting Hand is an entire system of thought that canine precognition has let us glimpse. What does it entail? That beneath any mass mediated surface appearance of generosity or kindness that the ruling powers (and this includes ruling powers of all sorts – political, economic, cultural, etc.) may evince toward the masses, there conspire hidden factions that actively seek to bring about the extinction of all human life and the extinction of all kindness" (Dramford 107).

Thus it is that the study of canid eschatology rarely offers comfort. It is not uncommon for those engaged in the field to require psychiatric care, to commit suicide, and to disappear from the face of the planet without the slightest trace. This is a scholarly subject with, pardon the pun, a wicked bite, and the oft-quoted Nietzschian aphorism "when you gaze long into an *abyss* the *abyss* also *gazes* into you" is never more appropriate than when one is churning through the undercurrents of deep canid eschatology. To undertake study of canid eschatology requires mental resolve and psychological resilience; it requires intelligence, sharpest scrutiny, and an open, creative mind. It is not for the weak. It is not for armchair philosophers. It is for those of us not afraid to stare upon the face of the end and describe its grim countenance to the rest of the world. I welcome all who believe themselves prepared for the challenge and remind them that Lyra Sciavalli, when she first conceived of her telepathy experiments so many years ago, couldn't possibly have known that she was about to break down a door to the future and stir widespread controversy. She couldn't possibly have known that our loyal canine companions were always already prophets of a darkening tomorrow. But this is precisely the point of the future: to veil "the fearful things, the bold new things, the things reaching out in love, and the things poised to strike a deadly blow." It just so happens that this veil may have been rent, long ago, by the baying of dogs. Now it is time for us to go exploring beyond the veil.

Mitchell D. Z. Gatz, Ph.D., Assistant Professor
Department of Canid Eschatology
Kelland University

References

Al-Hikmet, Azim. "The Unseen Violence of God: A New Interpretation of the Unpetting Hand." *Sciavalli's Children: Essays on the Canid Apocalyptic Visions in Lyra Sciavalli's Research.* Yale U.P.

Anusha, Priya. "A New Sense of Time: Boundaries of Canine Perception and Thought." *Speculative Frontiers* Vol. 16.1. pgs. 37-55.

Chaisson, Katrina. *Death in Many Breeds: The Apocalypses Awaiting Us within the Visions of Sciavalli's Dogs.* McFarland.

Dramford, K.L. *The Hand that Cuts Against Us All.* New Futures Press.

Headley, James. "Doggone Metaphors: A Rational View of Canine Prognostication." *Skeptical Digest* 39. pgs. 53-63.

Hertz, Clemens. "A Refutation of Precognition in Canidae." *Science Today* 129. pgs. 1-20.

Jameson, Miranda. "The Future is Not Theirs to See: An Interview with Rev. Bernard Hatfield." *U.S. News Weekly* Vol. 59, Issue 35. pgs. 36-44.

Matsuzaka, Yu. *Icarus Regards the Sun: The Personal Correspondence of Yu Matsuzaka.* Ed. Siobhan Greenfield. Oxford U.P.

Sciavalli, Lyra. *Alien Perceptions: The Inner Life of Dogs.* Knopf Doubleday.

—. *The Journals of Lyra Sciavalli*. Ed. Omar Mostapha. Harvard U.P.

—. "On the Potential for Interspecies Telepathy." *Journal of Exploratory Sciences* 31.2. pgs. 189-210.

The Unpetting Hand. Eds. Lyra Sciavalli, Priya Anusha, and Oliver Davids. Oxford U.P.

Dermatology, Eschatology

YOUR DOCTOR THINKS you have hives, but you know better. Hives are supposed to be red, not blue—a fact your doctor glossed over or purposely ignored—and you're not supposed to feel something moving inside your hives, which you do. You're afraid the real problem is insects. You're afraid a six-legged monster laid eggs under your skin and now its larvae are burrowing out. That's what the people online told you might happen, and it feels right. Or, more right than the doctor's diagnosis of hives, anyway.

As soon as you noticed the blue bumps running up and down your arms and your chest two weeks ago, you took to the Internet for answers. You wanted information, yes, but you also wanted to connect with other people who had similar afflictions. Misery loves company, says the old maxim, and the Internet is nothing if not a congregation of sorrow. So, you reached out on message boards and live chat apps and social media groups in an effort to find someone who could understand your illness. You wanted commiseration. You wanted friendship, however strangely formed. You wanted answers you could understand. And that's what you received, with an entomological bonus.

The people online asked for pics of your mottled skin and showed you pics of their ruined flesh in return. They mentioned flies and beetles and segmented things with razor pincers and toxic exoskeletons. They cited incidents where they'd had ticks suctioned to their bellies and ants latched onto their nether regions. They sent you links about egg sacs and pupae, sores, and wounds. They gave you the comfort that someone out there *did* care, if only as a member of the same neurotic society. These were people reaching out, trying to connect with you as you were trying to connect with them. That their explanations for your bumps were a little absurd only endeared them to you further. So, even though your doctor claims it's impossible, you think the potential for insect infection is worth consideration. At very least, it gives you a reason to go back online and chat about your worries.

When you arrive home after the doctor's visit, the movement within the blue bumps grows worse. You waste no time messaging the bug people on their message boards, their forums, their social media groups. You're looking for advice or further explanations or just a voice in the wilderness that proves you're not alone, but no one responds. It's the middle of the day. Everyone is probably busy with work. You keep posting, regardless. You want everyone to know the details of your appointment and your doctor's dismissive attitude. You're hoping for a little righteous anger on your behalf.

While you drop messages to your new wound-obsessed acquaintances, you scratch at the bumps. The longer you wait for responses, the more your scratching gains strength and traction. You refresh apps and web pages. You check messaging programs and your email. No one responds. Soon, you're no longer scratching, but clawing, and your fingers come away from your skin slicked with blood.

You don't panic, surprisingly, because this is an opportunity—an opportunity to see what lies inside those bumps, to give the people online even more information. You rush to the bathroom, wash away the blood from your arms and see, poking up from every torn bump, a cluster of silver wires.

Insects are nowhere to be found.

You touch one of the wire bundles, and it reacts, sliding further out of your ragged flesh and curling itself around your finger as though of its own volition. You pull your hand away, and the wire releases, but also continues to lengthen. It worms its way down the side of your arm and drops into the sink over which you're standing. There, it twitches as though conducting an electrical current.

You should be horrified, but you're thinking about all the ways to tell the people online. They're going to be so fascinated. They're going to be so jealous. You can't even imagine how much conversation this new development will generate.

Other exposed wires begin slinking from your body. They extend an arm's length from your body, twitching and flailing in midair. They seem to be seeking something, testing the surfaces with which they come in contact. Dozens of wire tendrils grow from you, wreathing you in a whipping chaos. You glance at the bathroom mirror, and you see a monster staring back. Or maybe it's a god.

Then again, maybe it's a dying animal.

A wave of dizziness and nausea sweeps over you. You decide this is all too much. It's not what you bargained for, exactly. It's too involved, too intense. Insects could be cleared up with some medications, a bit of lancing. But live wires sprouting from your skin? Well, no one online mentioned anything like that. What if it's too much for them, too? What if there's no one to understand this particular affliction? What if it drives them away from you? What if they won't talk to you anymore?

On the verge of passing out, you lie down in the middle of your bathroom. Your thoughts buzz—not like a fly or a bee, but like the sound of an overworked electrical outlet. You wish you could find some advice on your situation now more than ever. You wish you could reach out and contact someone, somewhere, who could lend perspective to the wires' emergence, but you don't imagine there is any such person. Still, you have to try. Somebody is out there. Somebody will care. Surely somebody will care.

Head lolling to the side, you search for your computer. You don't see it. You don't see anything except the lashing of wires all around you. It mesmerizes you with intricate weaves and patterns. Kaleidoscopic would be a way to describe it. Fractal, another. And as you watch the wires, entranced and overworked in body and mind, you fade out and enter a state wider than dreams and deeper than death. There, answers and connections and monstrosities are all irrelevant.

You wake to an untuned orchestra of screams. You try to sit up, but you can't. You're held fast by a network of wires, a spider caught in its own web. As you rested, the wires continued to grow and, horribly enough, multiply. They now sprout from every inch of your body. Every bundle of silver strands stretches into the distance, far beyond your field of vision. Some pass through the bathroom doorway. Some snake out of the broken bathroom window. A few have punched directly through the walls.

The screams continue. You realize they're not inchoate, but, rather, simply loud, and frightened. You try to isolate what they're saying. Among the fragments you pick out are:

"Get it out of me! Dear god, get it out!"

"Why can I hear all this?"

"It's gone straight through my chest! Straight through!"

"They're in my neck! They're moving!"

"How am I still alive? This should kill me."

and

"Who is that? Who's talking?"

You realize, all at once, that the voices aren't in your ears. They're in your head. They cry out in places far from your bathroom. But how? You consider the situation for a moment and come to a second, more terrible, knowledge: you can hear the voices because they're connected to you through the silver wires. You concentrate, and, somehow, as though through your own eyes, you see the wires where they puncture the screaming people, bundles of silver drilled into their flesh, leading directly from you to these frightened others. You see the shock, the awe. You see snarling mouths and tear-spotted cheeks and fingers probing at grievous wounds. And, of course, you see the wires, which wrap themselves around deep organs and bore through bone, entrails, and gray matter—anything that can be penetrated. No matter how deep they travel, the wires shoot back to the surface and pass out of their unwitting hosts, growing further, growing beyond, finding more bodies and minds to infiltrate, to knit together.

It's these people you hear, the people twisted up with you. You share their innermost thoughts; you pulse with their feelings. They're all connected to you, through you. A multitude, you ebb and flow as one. Thousands of people, maybe millions, lie elsewhere, impaled by the wires. They share this terror with you, united in pain and fear. You would tell them to relax, to let it happen, but you have no reason to believe this will end well.

Again, you try to move, but the weight of the wires and the many lives they now support is too great. No matter how much you strain, you can't lift your arms or legs more than a hair's breadth off the floor. How will you eat? How will you drink? Unless you can derive sustenance through the wires, this bathroom is where you will die. You wish you had your computer or your phone. The people online really need to hear about what's become of you. Alas, both remain far out of reach.

You wonder when—or if—the wires will stop growing and puncturing new victims. Will they continue on, even with your dry, desiccated corpse at their center? Will they encircle the world and everyone in it? Even now, are they seeking people halfway around the globe, in places you've never even heard of? You laugh, imagining the ridiculousness of an apocalypse that bloomed from your skin. Dermatology, eschatology—same difference, you think.

The screams reach a greater pitch. They need to be heard. They need to talk. To you. To each other. They need to share.

You laugh again. At least you've found a community that truly understands your plight and can sympathize. You're sure you'll all have a great deal to discuss in the time you have left.

Opus Manuum Artificis

. . . AND THE SPECTATORS remained silent, their faceless, egg-shaped heads swinging left-right-left-right like pendulums detached from alien clocks.

The curtain crept shut on the writhing, screaming exhibit before them, and they applauded, lank, needle-pointed fingers cracking hollow against one another. Unspoken praises and critiques passed among the onlookers. They moved on, floating to the next piece, a few dragging awkward pets in their wake.

As quickly as they left, so, too, another group of spectators glided into place and waited, blank, bleached heads marking seconds to infinity.

Behind the curtain, the stage was reset by unseen forces. The viewing would soon begin again.

Samuel Del Flaco's mouth was stapled shut.

He was certain it was staples.

His tongue could just barely squeeze between his chapped lips, and what it felt beyond was a series of cold, unyielding bars. When he had awoken here, in this unremarkable room, he'd attempted to yawn, but found that opening his mouth even a fraction of an inch resulted in a searing strike from tiny points of pain—seven just above his top lip and seven just below, if his count could be trusted. Sam's initial reaction had been to try to grab at the staples, as a child grasps at its toes for the first time. He needed to know the dimensions of these strictures, the nature of their substance, and the angles at which they were embedded. But discerning such facts was an impossibility, given that his hands were missing.

Sam held one arm out in front of him again. It ended at the wrist in a perfectly smooth, rounded stub. His hands were simply gone, severed somehow. There was no spurting wound, no ragged sutures or gangrenous gash. Not even a blister or a hint of scar tissue. The only reminder that some violence may have taken place was a muted lapping of discomfort across the length of his forearm, a dull burn, and even that was fading. It was as if his hands had simply melted away and left behind puddles of smooth, convex flesh.

Without hands, without fingers, there was no way to delicately explore the devices that held his mouth in check, let alone remove them. Brute force, and what was sure to be sweating, shredding agony, was the only immediate path to vocal freedom. Sam wasn't ready to consider that option yet. The staples would have to remain.

More pressing than his oral bondage, however, were the metal manacles clamped tightly around his ankles and his abdomen. He still had feet—a saving grace, perhaps—but they, like his stomach, were incarcerated beneath four inches of gleaming golden metal. Propped upon an equally gleaming golden table in a nearly standing position, Sam could have easily escaped from this room, had his naked form not been held fast by those three metal bands.

As he craned his neck in an effort to discern how the restraints were locked into place, a lance of hyperborean chill punctured his spine and sent a dull, rapacious ache rippling outward from an area just above his shoulder blades. He threw himself back against the table, jaw suddenly locked tight, and writhed like a worm cut in two. The pain—a blend of full-body frostbite and prizefighter kidney punches—gradually subsided and left Sam feeling as though he had been crushed beneath the ponderous tread of a glacier.

He took several deep breaths in an effort to assure himself that he was still dangling upon the mortal coil, then, with great finesse, began to feel about the base of his neck with the nubs of his wrists. Something was embedded in his back. He hadn't noticed it earlier because he hadn't really moved. But now, after experiencing its excruciating pressure, it was the center of his attention.

Even without fingers, Sam could feel two soft plastic tubes running into his body. Two tubes, but only one injection site: the tiny circle of torture that had alerted him to their presence in the first place. The tubes made him more uneasy than any other aspect of his predicament. He wasn't sure why. Maybe it was the fact that plastic tubes seemed such a conventional, pedestrian, and, most importantly, human invention.

Slowly, carefully, Sam twisted his torso until he could see, from the corner of his eye, where the tubes led. They snaked down, apparently through a hole cut out of the table, and into a massive, white, softly whirring machine that sat against the wall off to his left side. Though blurred in his peripheral vision, Sam was certain that it lacked any buttons, gauges, or digital displays; whatever its purpose, the machine's outward appearance was as little more than an unadorned, niveous cube.

Sam stared askance at the tubes that linked him to the whirring device. Within one flowed a dark crimson liquid—

blood?—while the other coursed with a sparkling, golden substance. Was this device pumping him full of healing elixirs or draining his life? The question picked at Sam's brain. Beads of sweat formed across his brow. He contemplated tearing the tubes from his back but abandoned the idea quickly; if simply jarring their port had sent him into near seizure, their forcible removal would surely kill him.

Untwisting and lying back against the surface of the table, panic began to slosh over the edge of a mental dam Sam hadn't even realized he'd built.

He wanted to scream, to fill the humming spaces of the room with a humane noise, but he knew that, given the rigidity of the staples joining his lips, such action would only lead to suffering and rent flesh. Instead, he tried to center himself and reflect. He needed to address basic questions, to battle sublime insanity with dry reason. How had he gotten here? Why was he here? And where was "here," anyway?

Although he found it difficult to focus while slogging through the mire of dread, Sam began to slowly stitch together memories from the loose images that dangled in his subconscious. He recalled drinking a pale, bubbly liquid—champagne or light beer, maybe—and eating white-frosted cake—coconut, if the ghost of flavor haunting his soft palate wasn't mere hallucination.

A sun-scorched blonde woman, who may or may not have been someone Sam once cared for, was weaved into the spaces between these culinary flashes. Strangely, something about her being was inflected with a wash of coconut, too. Sam remembered kissing this well-tanned woman at least once, but whether their lips met in love or lust or purely imaginary wish fulfillment, he didn't know.

Beneath the ephemera—the drink, the cake, the woman, the kiss—echoed an unbearable ringing as of a pistol shot in the cavernous chambers of some lower hell or a million glasses eternally toasting to prosperity and good health.

Sam didn't understand the connections his brain was trying to make. Stinging drops of perspiration began to drip into his eyes and the left side of his head began to burn as if prodded by the orange palm of a branding iron. Still, he clenched his teeth and forged on, doggedly patching his tattered past, determined to find answers for his current state.

Delving deep into the clutter of his mind, he managed to connect the impression of a gray-bearded man in a crisp black suit with a tense, whispered conversation. As with the blonde woman, the bearded man's identity was entirely absent from Sam's memory; he could have been Sam's father or his boss, his dearest friend or his most spite-filled enemy. The contents of their conversation were also wrapped in opaque abstraction. If Sam remembered correctly, their locutions had floated in orbit around vague concepts such as financial security and moral impropriety, but any exact phrases or proper names that might have tied these ideas to the phenomenal world were entirely missing. It was like reading a cartoon strip where the characters' speech bubbles were filled in with dollar signs and devil faces rather than words.

The bearded man. Money. Evil. Words, words, words. Then none. A fist. A crack. A scream. And blood. Blood. Blood everywhere. The blonde woman. Coconut. And blood everywhere.

As the flames beneath his skull licked higher and hotter and he teetered on the verge of potential stroke or aneurysm, Sam attempted to further penetrate his crumbled psyche.

He pushed past his sensorium, past the four-lobed inferno, and entered a cool, twilit, stone-laden chamber of once-upon times. Here, the ceiling sparkled, and the floor was less board or tile than billowy cloud. Ambiguous laughter erupted from unoccupied points in the room. Sam spun on his axis in the middle of the nebulous floor, a dancer engaged in eternal pirouette. Even though he could pinpoint no faces nor locate even a single body in the mist, he felt the chalky glimmer of thousand smiles trained upon him. And still he continued to spin. Before his eyes within eyes, the world melted into streaks of color and shapeless masses of sound. Was this a dream or a nightmare, a metaphor of experience or a heavily excised memory? There was no way to tell. Sam simply didn't have the mental stamina left to decipher his internal state and those impossible, foreign things which inhabited it. The fire in his head was too vast, too hungry; it lapped at reason and self, threatening to engulf all conscious thought. If he worked his singed neural pathways any longer, he was certain something would burst.

Taking a deep, labored breath, Sam returned to the world outside himself and stared up, into an impossible darkness, collecting what few shards of certainty he had left.

Gazing into the endless pitch, it seemed as if the room had no ceiling, but, rather, extended infinitely upward to places even gods spoke of in trembling tones, with the metal walls eventually evaporating into thick, pure nothingness. Sam turned his head to the side ever so slightly, careful not to disturb the port implanted in his neck, and looked in the opposite direction of the white, whirring machine.

There, slowly and sinuously undulating from an unseen and unfelt breeze, hung a shimmering, opalescent curtain. It glowed with the hue of distilled evenings and rippled like the tide of a reticent sea. Centuries passed as Sam stared at its wavering motion. Surely freedom and hope and all those things that radiated the tingling energies of possibility waited behind such a curtain. Surely this was a gateway that led back unto the realm of open lips and searching hands, where bodies were whole, and minds existed intact and knowing. Sam stretched his arm toward the glimmering fabric. It was so tantalizingly near, yet universes away. He tried to will an elastic extension of his arm but acts of willpower were of no consequence in this room.

As Sam held his nub-tipped limb aloft, beyond the boundaries of the steel table, a strand of soft, wet, almost lacy black material drifted down from the infinite tunnel above and landed on his bicep. Reaching across his chest, he prodded it with his opposite stump. The substance adhered to his flesh, sticking like an industrial epoxy. Sam tried to rub it with his nub-tipped arm, but it remained, unmoved and radiating crisp midnight darkness.

Then the dullness began to creep in.

From under the tarry matter spread ripples of analgesic emptiness, a numbing of not only nerve cells, but of the entire concept of "arm." It was as if something was erasing his limb from his mind, whitewashing his neurons and his senses, so that only a remote, vestigial memory of his arm remained. Sam rubbed harder, more furiously, the friction acting as his sole weapon against this all-pervasive loss. The skin surrounding the black strip turned pink, then red. Tiny crimson beads popped to the surface. Sam couldn't feel the damage he was inflicting upon himself, so thorough was the numbness. As he desperately tried to regain sensation by scrubbing his vital tissues away, another strand of black material drifted down from the inconceivable heights above. It landed, gently, like a longtime lover's touch, on his cheek.

Sam's live arm shot toward his face. At the same moment, a blizzard of dark confetti erupted from overhead; hundreds of strips of the strange anesthetic fell across Sam's chin, neck, and chest. In scant seconds, every patch of his exposed skin from mouth to midriff was swathed in airy darkness. A monolithic scream rolled from his throat and broke into muted pebbles against his stapled lips as the numbness stole over his upper body. Sam's eyes rolled upward, searching for a savior or, at very least, a feeling. Neither greeted his gaze. Rather, he beheld a massive something, a stolid bulk of even more permanent infinitude than the pitch which surrounded it, lumbering through the space above and, presumably, shedding these shards of desensitization.

Instinctively, Sam turned away, forgetting the tubes that pierced his back. The iced agony again shot through his spine, paralyzing those parts which hadn't already succumbed to the darkness. He bit down hard, his teeth coming together with a wet crack that sullied the antiseptic air of the room.

As he wrestled with pain, more confetti rained down from the lumbering thing and found final rest upon his forehead, nose, and mouth. Only his eyes remained uncovered.

Suddenly, the table upon which Sam reclined began to rotate. It spun ninety degrees, so that he now faced the glimmering curtain. Though Sam couldn't see it, preoccupied as he was with staving off the torturous force of the jarred port, one final strand of black material dropped from the shaft above. It fluttered through the air, twisting and—if such a thing were possible— hesitantly dropping with almost conscious deliberation. Simultaneously, as if skillfully designed to work in tandem with the material's slow descent, the curtain slid open. For brief minute, the pain receded, and Sam managed to glimpse what lay on the other side: a pane of tinted glass and, behind the glass, a crowd of vaguely human shapes. One of the figures stepped into a soft light that issued from somewhere behind the glass. It was the older, bearded man from Sam's memory, clothed in a dark suit and tie. A thick, green manacle was clamped around the man's neck and a heavy, rusted chain led off it, into the dimness beyond. The older man's eyes met Sam's. They bespoke nothing; they held no fire or ice, no love or hatred or even empathy, only distant recognition. Some deeper part of the bearded man than his mouth had, seemingly, been stapled shut.

A glint in the reflection off the glass caught Sam's attention. He squinted to find its source. As best he could tell, the reflection came from a spectacularly shiny plate beneath his feet. Barely visible words were engraved upon its surface. Squinting even harder, straining to the point of near macular rupture, Sam read, backward, the phrase that framed his circumstance: "Opus Manuum Artificis." He didn't know what any of the words meant, though they looked like something he might've heard during a Catholic mass. Again, he glanced at the older man, perhaps for answers or perhaps because there was no one else to return his gaze.

Without warning, the chain leading off the older man's metal collar drew taut, and he was dragged from the light. Another figure moved into his place. Sam forgot the plaque beneath him and stared, the hair on his still-sensate arm standing at attention. While the being that now stood in the bearded man's place had two arms, two legs, and wore a conventional suit and tie, it lacked a human head. Instead, what rested atop its shoulders was a chalky white ovoid without any distinguishing features; it swiveled from side to side rhythmically, a pale metronome keeping time in a vacuum. As Sam stared through the glass, watching the thing observe him, the final strip of dark confetti finally landed, falling across Sam's eyes as if with a measure of meticulous calculation, its sticky, silken surface blotting out any further view of his spectators.

Sam didn't struggle against the blinder; numbness had already excavated the life from his upper body. He was a mummy wrapped in night, preserved for a perilous journey toward eternity. The disparate valleys and nodes of his brain that coalesced into one unified "Sam" were sinking under a flood of stultifying, inky laminate. The phenomenal Sam—the dynamic, thinking, feeling, and doing Sam with scattered memories and confusion in his heart—began to dissolve. Sam twisted and turned, though he could not feel it. He screamed and tore all the staples from his mouth, but neither did he feel the sear of splitting flesh nor the blood gushing from his ragged lips.

"Sam" was gone. All that remained propped on the silver table was a moment, a slice of man forever trapped in the blink of the present.

The things beyond the curtain approved.

Sam awoke to a gentle whir. He was lying on a table tilted upright at nearly forty-five degrees. He had no clue where he was or how he'd arrived at this place. The only explanation was circumstance, whether fated or chanced.

Groggy and dislocated, Sam began to yawn, but a series of sharp, serrated tugs on his lips prevented his mouth from opening. His hands flew upward, seeking out the source of his distress. He stretched his fingers toward the pain and realized, absurdly, that his fingers were missing; in fact, his entire hand was gone. The tips of his arms ended in smooth, rounded flesh mounds, as if he were a hastily sketched caricature whose hands had simply been erased.

He looked at his stubs, confusion and fear slipping and sliding into one another in his mind. He began to sputter "What the hell?" but the phrase died on his tongue. Spread out beyond his deformed arms, his nude body lay trapped by a series of metal bands—one thick and tight against his waist and two clamped securely about his ankles.

He breathed deeply. *One problem at a time*, he thought. *If I can figure out what's on my mouth and remove it, I can call out for help.*

Raising a nub to his lips, he felt along their length. Dry, cracked skin was interrupted by hard, penetrating bars at equal intervals.

Samuel Del Flaco's mouth was stapled shut.

He was certain it was staples...

A Plague of the Most Beautiful Finery

THE ODOR THAT slithered through the gap between the boxcar's doors stopped Grimble's heart long before he saw the bodies. Threads of rot and wine, blood and fine cologne, excrement and crisp linen all knitted together in the scent's fabric. As its arachnoid limbs twisted toward his nostrils, Grimble turned away, flipped on his flashlight, and glanced at the shipping manifest in his hands.

Box number US-2018: Paper goods and industrial air conditioning parts. No perishables. No chemicals. Nothing that would explain the pungent smell.

Fifteen years in the train yard, fifteen years of thankless midnight inspections, and Grimble had never caught a whiff of something like this. He knew the stench of dead animals, the musk of mold and mildew, the tang of acids and oils and solvents of unnamable variety. But this odor, this was something new. This was something that, considering the car's broken lock and ajar doors, had to be investigated.

Grimble set his stack of paperwork on the ground, breathed deep, and opened a nightmare.

His flashlight beam swiveling throughout the inside of the boxcar revealed a mound of nude, gray, desiccated bodies. Around the perimeter of the car, on nails driven into the walls, hung maybe two dozen clean, pressed, impeccably tailored blue suits replete with white button-down shirts and apple-red ties.

Grimble dropped the flashlight, which lolled about inside the car, and whispered, more to whatever gods would listen than to himself, "No. No. Not here. Not now."

Something soft rustled in the darkness just outside the flashlight's reach and Grimble fled. Unfurling a carpet of expletives in his wake, he grabbed for the phone in his pocket and dialed 9-1-1.

A bored, wispy voice answered.

"9-1-1. What's the nature of your emergency?"

Not used to exercise, let alone full-on sprinting, Grimble panted into his phone, "The suits. The suits. They're not contained. They're here. Middleton train yard. The suits are here."

"Sir? You're reporting an outbreak? Are you a railroad employee?"

"Yes! Yes!" Grimble shouted. "Middleton train yard. The suits."

"I understand, sir. I'm forced to ask, what is your yearly salary? Do you have enough money to placate the suits?"

Chest heaving, Grimble had no breath with which to respond. He grunted at the phone and kept running. Thirty thousand plus benefits would be no salvation here. The suits had never been known to spare anyone with less than six digits-worth of earning power to their name.

Behind Grimble, out of sight, the dread pathogen rushed over the tracks, its movement silent but for an occasional swish of cloth against cloth.

"Sir? We've never had a report this far northwest. Are you certain they're the plague suits?"

Grimble could see the station master's office glowing in the distance. Heart dancing wildly, he choked out as much information as he could.

"Yes. They're following. Came from inside a train car. Twenty. Thirty. Dead inside."

A silhouette came into focus just outside the office. It was one of the mechanics, Hardesty, walking toward the repair building, hammer in hand.

"Get inside!" Grimble screamed.

Hardesty stopped and stared in confusion, then began jogging in Grimble's direction.

"No! No! Go ins..." Grimble's warning dissipated as he tripped on a high-rising track and collapsed to the ground.

Dazed, knees and elbows bruised and bleeding, he heard two distinct noises nearby: one, the thud of Hardesty's steel-toed boots pounding closer and, two, a ripple of cotton and wool rushing forth like a tidal wave.

Grimble's phone lay several feet away, still connected to the 9-1-1 operator.

"Sir? Are you there? I'm sending fire and quarantine units. If you can hear me, try to surround yourself with as much currency as possible. Paper money, credit cards, checks, an open bank account app on your phone—anything you can lay your hands on. You might confuse them. Remember, they won't take people who have the scent of wealth on them."

Ignoring the phone, Grimble stumbled to his feet and set his bulk to push forward. He rushed by Hardesty, who scowled in confusion.

"Grimble, what the fu..."

The hungry slither of silk devoured Hardesty's words.

Grimble chugged onward, even as a series of wet cracks echoed from where Hardesty had been overtaken.

The office was so close. So close.

Finally back in the halogen glow of the terminal's lights, Grimble dared a glance over his shoulder and saw what he'd feared he might: two, maybe three dozen suits still perfectly flat and starched, floating toward him. Their ties stood out from their shirts and jackets, undulating slowly in an unfelt breeze, tasting the atmosphere for poverty and desperation.

Grimble shivered and kept moving. The door was within an arm's length. He reached out and pulled. Nothing happened. Locked. Locked out of the office. Locked out of safety.

Grimble whirred about on his heels. The suits were there, floating nearer, nearer, their cuts magnificent, their lapels sharp, their pocket squares—also red—neatly folded and pointing up, at a sky of indifferent stars.

Grimble reached into his back pocket, drew forth his wallet, and threw his ATM card at one of the suit's breasts. His name and account number bounced away into the night.

He pulled out a credit card and brandished it before him like a crucifix before the undead. Another suit, now fully upon Grimble, reached out and, with a solid albeit empty arm, slapped the plastic ward from Grimble's hand.

Devoid of any more potential weapons, Grimble heaved his entire wallet—full of dollar bills and frequent customer cards, identifications, and insurance proofs—into the massing livery.

They ignored the pittance and focused instead on Grimble's body, tie-tongues waving hello and goodbye. Grimble slouched to his knees and let them come. He had no means to fight this plague. He possessed nothing they wanted except his life.

Soon enough, his neck would be snapped in a tie's red noose. Soon enough, they would carry him away. And soon enough, he would be riding a boxcar, naked and bloated, brought to his final resting place by a plague for which there was no cure but fire, a plague of the hollowest, most stylish, most beautiful finery.

Grimble set his jaw, closed his eyes, and, with the pride of a dying class, waited for the suits to strike.

Pwdre Ser

If you've ever watched the night sky you know that all sorts of things hurtle through it, burning and spinning from one edge of nowhere to another. You also know that sometimes one of those celestial wanderers loses its way and lands in our laps, its arrival unexpected and mysterious, full of wonder and a threat so vague we barely care to call it a threat. Thus it was with the glob that crashed through the ceiling of King High School on the day of our town's centennial celebration.

We'd been preparing for the centennial for nine months and, by the time of its arrival, believed that we'd birthed an event of such vast historical magnitude and cultural import that we convinced our local public-school board to declare a formal holiday for all students, faculty, and staff. The carnival, the parade, the speeches by town council members and elderly denizens: it was all deemed sufficiently educational to fit through a loophole in our state's policy on attendance. So, when the glob exploded into King High School and obliterated Ms. Mahfouz's social studies classroom, blowing out walls and blasting shrapnel hundreds of meters from the building, we lost not a single member of our town to its deadly concussive wave.

At the time, we counted ourselves lucky and thanked the stars for smiling upon us with so much favor. But now, nearly a year later, with half our population missing and the other half descended into a state akin to madness, one might contend that the stars did not smile that day. Instead, perhaps they whispered a word to us, a word we are far too simple to comprehend and far too weak to retain for our own vocabularies, a word that has consumed us, a word we can only loosely translate as "jelly."

The Town

We live in a small town that crouches at the lonely end of a peninsula which, at its base, sprouts off into a much larger peninsula. On our every side lurch the sluggish tides of a defeated sea and beneath our feet stretch loose soils that remain spongy and warm year-round. A wild array of dense grasses and prehistoric shrubs sprout eternal from every unpaved inch of ground and engage us in a never-ending battle for control of the land. Mosquitos large as hummingbirds and roaches girded by steel plating invade our homes with casual aplomb. Because we lie entirely too near the equator, the temperature in our town fluctuates little, a fact of life which provides us with only two distinct seasons: Balmy and Blistering. Meanwhile, above us, a confluence of powerful jet streams prevents our town from becoming overly familiar with cloudy days but also assures that we experience a full month of biblical deluge every August.

One might assume that this geographical and climatological assignment, with its supposed subtropical enchantments, would mean that our town maintains a thriving tourism industry or, at least, the potential for such. But one would be wrong. The exotic idylls of sand and surf have never been a part of our lives. We have beaches on our peninsular purgatory, true, but they are less oases of finely-ground white sand than spits of dislocated seaweed paved by fragmented, razor-edged mollusk shells. The gulf beyond those beaches is an equally inhospitable gray expanse. Teeming with sharks, jellyfish, and spiny urchins, it neither swells high enough to interest water sports enthusiasts nor hides a sufficient diversity of game fish to entice anglers. Thus it is that our substantial shoreline has never attracted much attention from the vacationing set, and we have remained, for better or worse, a relatively isolated community dedicated to citrus farming and the industrial manufacture of patio furniture. We are, at bottom, a town of castaways.

It should come as no surprise, then, that our insular little community has always valued its traditions, whether ceremonial, functional, or nonsensical. Every year, for instance, we crown a Grapefruit Queen during the winter harvest festival, and every year we invite local high schools to participate in a Battle of the Marching Bands competition during our Memorial Day parade. In the summer we set up a town fair replete with pie eating contests and ring toss booths, and in the fall, we hold a Samhain celebration with a bonfire and free orange juice. These traditions bind us together and remind us that although we are seemingly cloistered away at the tip of the world and lack the bustling charms of a seaside resort, there are far worse places we could be. Perhaps this is why the centennial was of such significance—it was a celebration of the very concept of "us" and our collective perseverance in the face of a world that countenances us with complete and utter apathy when it countenances us at all.

The Celebration

We spared no expense in organizing the centennial celebration. Held precisely one-hundred years to the day after our town's founding, it was to be a full twenty-four hours of revelry. We booked a host of bands to play in our town's tiny amphitheater from dawn until midnight, and we invited all manner of food trucks to ply their delicacies along our streets. We presided over various games of skill and chance—with their proceeds donated to local charities, of course—and we arranged for a fireworks display after dusk. We hired off-season carnies to set up and operate a thoroughfare of dizzying rides and arranged for local artists to create a pop-up gallery on the festival grounds. We even enticed a consortium of small brewery owners to provide free beer tastings throughout the day. By the time the celebration kicked off, our downtown looked more the part of a busy amusement park than the crosshatch of four pothole-laden streets it truly is—a fact that greatly pleased us.

We inaugurated the event with the unveiling of a life-size, bronze replica of our town's seal—essentially, a man and woman shading their eyes from the sun as they gaze skyward—in the town square. The ceremony drew a surprisingly large crowd, which only grew thicker as the morning wore on and the real celebration commenced. Children scampered between rides, their faces alight with the joy of an unexpected reprieve from school and their fingers sticky with sugary treats they'd cajoled their parents into purchasing for them. Teenagers reclined in the vicinity of the bands, alternately dancing to the music, and ducking behind the amphitheater's stage to take pulls from travel-sized bottles of liquor they'd swiped from their parents' cabinets. Adults gorged themselves on food and drink from the congregated vendors, played the games we'd devised (more as a point of friendly competition with one another than because they wanted the prizes), and tried to wrangle their children, if children they had. The elderly strolled the downtown thoroughfare with leisurely grace and eventually settled in a temporary pavilion we'd constructed for the festival's bingo tournament. It seemed our entire community had allowed itself a gleeful vacation day to indulge in the pleasures of the centennial celebration. It seemed all was well, and all would always be well, so long as we could find togetherness in our mutual alienation. Thus, the celebration cartwheeled along until, early in the afternoon, the sky split open and bled disaster upon us.

At first, we didn't even know anything had gone awry. We didn't recognize the widening gash above us any more than we might recognize a flittering mote at the corner of our eyes. Gradually, however, some of our arms began to stretch outward and upward, fingers pointing to the zenith of the cloudless firmament; some of our faces began to tilt ninety degrees from their conventional angles of repose; and some of our feet began to root themselves to the ground where they stood. Soon, all our cavorting halted, and we took up the mantle of the awestruck. The music from the amphitheater died, and the burble of our collective voices diminished to a sallow breeze of whispers. Childlike questions sprang from our tongues: "What is it? What should we do? Have you ever seen anything like that?" Too right these questions were, for the phenomenon that drew our attention could only be evaluated by the most fundamental of interrogatories. None of us—neither the oldest nor the wisest nor the most learned among us—had ever seen anything like the tear in the sky that loomed over our town: a wide strip of radiant red light along the length of which ran a thin, opalescent line. It reminded us of an inflamed wound clotted by auroras. It reminded us how far from the rest of the world we really were.

As we stared at the fulgent split above, phones and cameras slowly rising to snap pictures, a commercial passenger plane passed high over our town. We feared that the plane would be sucked into the aerial disturbance—whatever it might be—and destroyed. But it wasn't. Instead, it continued its flight without incident, disappearing for a few seconds when it reached the tear but reemerging on the tear's opposite side without apparent damage or distress. The reason for the plane's unhindered progress puzzled us. Were we mass hallucinating the rift in the sky? Was it nothing more than an optical illusion?

We worried over our sanity and our fragile perceptions for several tense minutes until, finally, a particularly astute woman in the crowd shouted, her voice wavering, "The plane went over. It was higher than that thing up there. That thing is low. Really low. And it's right over us." These words lodged a peculiar dread at the base of our skulls, a dread that sent all rational thought scurrying for cover. We were granted no time to explore the consequence of this fear, though, because a matter of seconds after the woman stopped speaking, the opalescent line at the center of the gash quivered and a silvery, ovoid object emerged from its depths.

The object arced away from the tear and began to rapidly descend toward our town. Reactions to the descent varied. Some of us sprinted to the nearest concrete or brick structure and hid within its walls. Some of us dropped to our knees and began to pray. Some of us even began to weep. The majority of us simply stood paralyzed in the festival grounds, our eyes bulging, our mouths agape, and the hair on our arms raised in a strangely satisfied sort of alarm. We realized disaster was approaching—inevitable disaster, spectacular disaster, disaster of the sort that prefigures marble memorials and award-winning documentaries—but we held absolutely no power to prevent it. When a god decides to throw a punch to your jaw, there's no illusion of dodging; there's just the awe of the fist, blasting numinous promises on the leading edge of its knuckles. So, as the object hurtled ever closer, the importance of our centennial dissipated.

Nearer and nearer it screamed, growing larger in our sight—clearly the size of a small van, if not bigger—but no more distinct, remaining a silvery blotch on the empyrean canvas. We couldn't determine where it would hit when it finally touched ground and, bizarrely, in our sublime moment of anticipation, we didn't particularly care. Fear and wonder had entirely filled us, driving out concern for much of anything beyond the object and its potential destructive power. Thus it was that we did little else other than stare as the object rushed overhead and slammed into the horizon.

When it landed, it sent up a concussive pop—a sound that seemed to us too delicate, too fragile for the import with which we'd imbued its arrival. And yet, the pop reverberated in our skulls. Though we couldn't explain how, we seemed to sense where the object had collided with our town. Our internal compasses orienting themselves to ground zero, we began to move in the direction they pointed. Those of us who had been praying quickly thanked our gods and took up behind the train toward the crash site. Those of us who had run for shelter returned to the flowing crowd with a flush of embarrassment and downcast glances. We welcomed all to the massing herd.

With a singularity of purpose we could not grasp, we tromped off toward the silvery thing from the sky and, before long, our downtown sat entirely vacant of life, our valued centennial celebration—if not officially then certainly in practice—canceled in lieu of spectacle.

The Jelly

The entire populace of our town seemed to arrive at the locus of the object's impact—King High School—simultaneously, as though we had been called by a voice heard in the very flow of our blood. By foot, by car, by bicycle and skateboard, we pulled up to the school and gawked at the severity of its wounds. Though the structure had been designed to withstand hurricane-force winds, one of its outer walls had partially collapsed, scattering glass, cinderblock, and concrete chunks onto both its lawn and the public road that ran adjacent to it. A ragged cavity pocked the center of the collapsed portion of the wall, and it was to this cavity that we were drawn.

Cutting paths through the rubble of slivered desks and battered textbooks that had been hurled from the school, we forged our way into the hole and began to seek out remnants of the object that had wrought so much damage. Surprisingly, local firefighters, police officers, and paramedics who had rushed to the scene didn't prevent us from our ingress—indeed, they joined us in our march and helped clear away jagged bits of wall that may have otherwise made entering the gap in the wall a dangerous proposition.

We didn't know why we wanted to enter the ruined schoolroom so desperately, nor did we understand what we would do once we'd found purchase there. We simply felt that we must go in, that the object, whatever it may have been, had carried with it some sort of essential revelation. So, into the breach we stumbled, congregating nearly shoulder to shoulder within the blasted hollow of what had, only minutes before, been a richly stocked storehouse of knowledge.

Inside the classroom—now barely recognizable as such—we shoved and jostled for position to reach the object's impact crater, a circular patch of broken concrete and dislodged topsoil roughly five feet in diameter. A subtle antiseptic odor issued from the crater and put us in mind of syringes and scalpels and hospital corridors. As we neared the lip of the depression, we saw that something rested at its nadir—a bulbous, bright red mass, translucent but for tiny pinpoints of silver embedded throughout its whole. We crept down, into the crater, and several of us prodded the mass with the tips of our shoes and detritus from the explosion that we'd picked up along the way. The mass responded with only a slight jiggle. On a hunch that it might have been permeable, someone in the crowd drove a pointed shard of broken whiteboard into its topmost pole. The shard passed into the mass without resistance. A different hand pulled the whiteboard shard back out, and it retracted just as easily, seemingly devoid of any residue.

"It's like a lump of jelly," someone at the precipice of the crater said. "Sky jelly." Many susurrations of assent drifted up from the crowd. We could think of the mass in no other terms, almost as though it had named itself. More, we now knew what we had to do.

Those of us on the fringes of the room dispersed throughout the school and began a frantic search, picking up coffee mugs from the faculty lounge and janitorial buckets from supply closets, plastic cups from the cafeteria and glass beakers from science labs. We returned to the crash site with these and other concave items in tow and distributed them evenly, so that, before long, every one of us held a container capable of transporting liquids. It then became a simple matter to satiate the desire that squirmed at the base of our brains—the desire that said "Take the jelly. Protect the jelly. Cherish the jelly."

One by one, we dipped our cups and mugs and buckets deep into the bulging jelly bubo and filled them to their brims. Then away we fled. We stumbled from the crash site in a daze, our sundry containers clutched tightly to our breasts. We protected the jelly as one might protect an expensive wine or a rare perfume or a draught of water from the fountain of youth. We made sure not to spill a single lump to the ground, speeding to our homes as quickly as possible so that we could secure the jelly in safer vessels. By evening, we had emptied the impact crater of its contents entirely. As we scampered from the broken school, exceedingly few of us bothered to look up at the gash in the sky that had provided the precious jelly. The handful of us who did glance upward saw that the tear had vanished as mysteriously as it had appeared, almost as though it had never existed in the first place.

The Calls

The first week after we'd scooped the jelly from the crater turned out to be the strangest span of time any of us could recall—at least, to that point in our lives. Cell phone reception within our town limits dropped to near zero, and telecommunication land lines experienced long periods of inexplicable frying noise. Traffic signals throughout town shorted out, and our streetlights began glowing an eerie pale red rather than their usual lightning blue. Our pets growled at spaces in our homes where no obvious threats showed themselves. Our children and our elderly woke in the deepest pitch of night, complaining of nightmares and visions of "wobbly, stretched out people." Even the gray waters that surrounded us seemed ill at ease, cresting high and hard despite clear weather.

Amidst the slowly swelling dysphoria, some of us received abnormal—if not wholly frightening—messages. Although our phones had been rendered nearly inoperable following the jelly's arrival, a smattering of calls did make their way both to and from us. It was during these rare, connected calls that the messages trickled through.

Carmilla Maldonado, proprietor of our town's sole bookstore, was the first to be contacted. She said that while she was on the phone with an insurance agent, discussing premiums for her business for the next year, "the connection clicked four or five times in rapid succession and a sound—something like wind rushing through a tunnel—took over the line. Under the sound, whatever it was, I could make out a voice, a woman's voice, husky and strained, halfway between screaming and moaning. I'd never heard anything like it outside of maybe a horror movie. This woman on the phone, she was repeating a series of words over and over. I thought maybe she was being abused or was having a medical emergency, so I asked her 'Can I help you? Can I help?' but she didn't answer. I listened close, trying to pick out her words from beneath the rushing noise in my ear. When I finally managed to understand what she was saying, it turned every drop of blood inside me to ice. This woman, she was screaming and moaning and tearing up her throat wailing, 'My baby. My baby is gone. My baby. My baby is gone.' I wanted to ask her what had happened. I wanted to ask her if I could call someone for her or if she needed to talk. But I couldn't find the words. I was too shocked. So I sat there listening for a while. Then the phone clicked again, and the call disconnected and there was only silence, which, in its way, was almost worse than the screaming had been. That silence, there was something disturbing in it, something wanting, something reaching out with an extremely sharp need. My skin crawls just trying to imagine what that need might have been."

Others among us received similarly bizarre calls with similarly bizarre messages later that first week. During a phone conversation with a patient regarding test results, Jared Moon, a nurse in one of our town's three doctor's offices, was interrupted by, in his words, "really heavy distortion and a really deep voice that growled something like 'It is all lost.'" Trix Beleaux, vice-principal at the damaged King High School, had her office voicemail filled with, as she put it, "dozens of messages that sounded as though they'd been made from inside a hurricane. Every one of them said the same thing, but in different tones and pitches and volumes. Every one of them said, 'Let them bleed.'"

Even 9-1-1 operators experienced unexplained telephonic interjections. Taliya Smith, one of those operators, explained that the call that disturbed her most wasn't a message at all, but, in her estimation, "a noise like you'd get if you took two pieces of rusty metal about the size of planets and scraped them back and forth over each other. It was such a huge, distant, lonely sound. It made me want to wrap myself up in blankets and pray for strength."

We should have been more attentive to these mystery messages and the other odd signs we received. We should have wondered what they might mean, what they might portend. We should have been concerned—or, at the least interested—that they occurred at all, that such strange buds were blooming in our town. But the jelly held us completely mesmerized, monopolizing our attentions and our thoughts.

As evidence of this monopolization, every household in our small community had placed its allotted jelly in a position of prominence, if not honor. Crystal decanters, silver urns, gold-plated goblets, antique cigar tins and music boxes: any family heirloom or expensive tchotchke that might reasonably contain liquid without spillage was put to use in service of the jelly. On our mantelpieces and in the centers of our dining room tables we displayed these vessels, making certain that their precious contents might be seen by passersby as frequently as possible. Every day, we gathered our families around the jelly and quietly basked in its glitter for hours, entering something akin to a meditative Zen state or a religious fugue. We broke our reverential silences only to ask questions such as "Is it alive?" and "Can we touch it?"—questions we weren't sure we wanted answered definitively, in truth. The draw of the jelly was so strong that many of us even burned our sick days and our vacation time from work just so we could stay home and stare into the sparkling red blobs we'd collected. We were a primitive people discovering fire, and all we wanted to do was sit in awe and watch it flicker.

The Initial Cost

Weeks passed. Though our phones still experienced a bevy of problems with dropped calls and poor connectivity, we received fewer and fewer unexplained messages. As the calls dwindled, however, the establishment of routines surrounding the jelly increased—routines that, for all intents and purposes, shaped and reshaped our lives.

In some homes, every member of the household rubbed the jelly's container before setting off for work or school and rubbed the container again upon returning home. In other homes, family members spent a few minutes before every meal to express their admiration for the jelly and briefly explain its positive impact upon their day. In still other homes, each person in the house privately whispered their hopes and dreams to the jelly just before lying down for a good night's rest.

Some of the routines we formed caused more significant shifts in our behavior. For instance, in an effort to further glorify the jelly we continually upgraded its domicile, draining our bank accounts to provide it with goblets forged from ever more precious metals, boxes studded with jewels of increasing quantity and purity, and decanters cut in progressively complex shapes with a finer degree of precision. It was also not uncommon to see people in our town wearing tiny glass vials suspended from gold and silver chain necklaces—glass vials into which they'd placed single drops of jelly, so as to keep it near to their hearts. No fewer than five distinct groups met in our local library on a biweekly schedule in order to study the jelly and discuss its meaning in their individual members' lives. The boldest among us even incorporated the jelly into our sex lives, though the details of such activities are best left to the realm of fantasy.

While our relationships with the jelly flourished, however, our town, as a unified organism, seemed to retract within itself. Fewer and fewer cars passed by on our streets. Our shops and restaurants sat vacant of customers. Bars closed by nine. The wind played over childless playgrounds and swept clean empty sidewalks. Intramural sports leagues dissolved; youth activities went unattended. We shunned television, radio, and all but the shallowest inlets of the Internet's information sea. Many of us began to refuse visits from family and friends who didn't live in our town, as we feared that they might not understand the jelly's importance or, worse, that they might steal it away from us. When not at work or school, we huddled in our homes, bound to our jelly, desperate to be near it.

To say that the jelly had become a fixture in our world would have been an understatement. It dominated our thoughts and our movements as few people or things ever had or ever would. It provided tangible evidence that we were different and special. And, most important of all, it bestowed on us a sneaking suspicion that we were not as alone as we had always thought.

The Wobbly People

Had we listened to our children and our elders, we might have been prepared. We might have intuited that the voices that had invaded our phones *en masse* had been but a single cog spinning revolutions in service of some sort of greater machine. We might have even conceived of a plan to deal with future intrusions. But, like innumerable generations before us, we didn't listen to our children or our elders. When they complained that wobbly, rubbery people were leering at them through their bedroom windows and stalking the sidewalks of our town in their nightmares, we brushed their fears aside as byproducts of overactive imaginations. We rubbed their shoulders and ensured them that wobbly, rubbery people didn't exist outside their windows or anywhere else. We brought the jelly to their bedrooms and held their hands as we led them in contemplation of the starlight refracted in the jelly's pinpoint sparkles. We fed them cookies, decaffeinated tea, anti-anxiety medications, and told them, "It's okay. We'll all be okay. No one pays us any mind, especially not weird wobbly people." And we were right.

Until we weren't.

While we obsessed over the jelly, our forgotten streets came alive without us.

A man speeding home from his second shift janitorial job and thinking of nothing but the jelly waiting for him in a stained-glass box on his bedroom windowsill saw what he described as "a person that was way too tall, like they were on stilts, milling around on the lawn in front of King High School."

A woman taking her dog for a midnight bathroom break and dreaming of new spatial placements for the jelly in her den witnessed what she believed to be "a person with really long arms staggering along on the sidewalk on the opposite side of the street from my house, like they had just spent a hundred years on a boat and couldn't find the right way to walk on land just yet."

A group of teenagers meeting after dark on one of our decrepit beaches to share a joint and muse on the hypothetical effects of smoking the jelly said that they encountered "two people with necks as long as a person's forearm just sort of swaying in the scrub by the beach and making really low-pitched noises that almost sounded like a chant in a foreign language."

A pair of convenience store clerks waxing philosophical about the supreme incorruptibility of the jelly as they worked their graveyard schedule observed, in their words, "a person with spider arms and legs rocking back and forth in the shadows along the edge of the store parking lot, like a cobra does before it strikes."

On and on the sightings rolled. Page three of our local newspaper became a repository of letters to the editor detailing encounters with the wobbly, elongated people. Rumor-hungry friends and neighbors group-texted us new reports of shadowy strangers throughout the day, every day. We couldn't even share a cup of coffee with our co-workers without the ensuing break time conversation reluctantly but necessarily shifting from jelly to wobbly invaders.

Yet, for all our newfound attention to the wobbly people, we didn't yet sense any overt menace in the sightings. It's true that we felt a thickening in the air and a deeper whisper in the palm fronds beyond our windows when the breeze would blow, but we didn't suspect it augured doom. Perhaps the jelly had occluded our vision. Perhaps we had intentionally let it flow into our eyes. Perhaps blindness had been its greatest gift to us all along. Whatever the reason, we felt certain that, were protection of our community necessary, the jelly would, somehow, protect us.

We were, of course, proven wrong.

The Knock

Exactly four months to the day from the jelly's immaculate collision with our town, Danielle Cinder, a guidance counselor at King High School, and her ten-year-old son Drake received a rapid-fire knock on their front door just as they sat down for a late dinner. Danielle, startled and expecting no guests, tiptoed to the door to answer, but saw no one standing on the stoop outside her home when she glanced through the door's peephole. Assuming the knock had been nothing more than neighborhood children playing a joke or a tired missionary bearing religious tracts, she had just turned to resume her place at the dinner table when another knock machine gunned the door. She spun back to the peephole and, from that vantage, spotted an exceptionally long-fingered hand snaking out of the shadows beyond her porch—a hand, which, by her estimate, must have measured two feet from the tip of its index finger to the base of its palm. She locked the door's deadbolt and waited at the peephole, watching as the hand twitched and twisted in the air with an unnamable palsy. Though she considered turning on the front porch light, Danielle decided that she had no desire to glimpse the trunk from which the monstrous hand had budded.

Danielle stood transfixed in terror by the hand's chaotic gyres. She could neither flee with her son—who quietly repeated "Who is it, mom?" between forkfuls of macaroni and cheese—nor could she open wide the door and face her visitor. So she waited, and, as she waited, a voice beyond the door began to crackle and spit like a flare stoked in an endless cavern. "It needs to be one," the voice said. "It needs to be one. Return it or reflect it."

Whether wisely or foolishly, Danielle refused to answer, setting her back against the door and hoping the unsettling visitor would leave. After cycling through its phrases nearly a dozen more times, this hope was fulfilled, as the voice melted into the stillness of the evening and disappeared, along with the elongated hand that carried it.

Stories of Danielle's contact with one of the wobbly people quickly spread throughout our town, setting our nerves on edge. Surely, we confided to our families, she had been wrong about the nature of the visitor. Surely the hand had been a rubber plaything from a Halloween store and the voice nothing more than that of a prankster out for a lark. Surely, we whispered into the jelly when no one else was around, the wobbly people would leave us alone and cause us no harm. We understood that our town's once-impermeable shell had sustained a crack, yet we refused to believe it might widen and split us asunder.

No amount of disbelief, however, halted any of the close encounters of the elongated kind that were to come.

The Visitations

Less than a week after the knock on Danielle Cinder's door, a pair of nearly eight-foot-tall women wearing diaphanous black cloaks called on Stanley Hillson, an accountant at our town's patio furniture factory, while he slept. It was just after midnight and Stanley had been wading deep in dreams when he was woken by loud rapping on his second-floor bedroom window. Shaking himself into the conscious world, he stumbled from his bed and looked through his window, outside of which he beheld the women—two virtual giantesses—standing on his condo's tiny lawn. They stared up at Stanley without any expression, their faces held so rigid that Stanley's first impression of the women was that they might be gigantic department store mannequins. This notion was dispelled only when they swung their arms, which were nearly the length of their entire bodies, up to the bedroom window and again rapped on the pane. Stanley, unnerved by the unnatural proportions of the women's limbs, drew shut the window's blinds and returned to his bed, where he pulled his sheets tight about his neck. He tried to fall back to sleep, but the women on the lawn didn't leave until near dawn—a span of time during which Stanley claimed that he intermittently heard more tapping on his window and whispers from outside that said, "Let it come back to the sky. Let it come back to the sky."

Two days later, Julia Esperanza, an EMT with the ambulance service in our town, had just finished a late shift at work when she received a visit from a man with a head as long as his torso. At roughly twelve-thirty, as Julia pulled into her driveway following her shift, her car's headlights revealed a figure teetering about in front of her garage. Clad in a garment Julia could only describe as a black turtleneck five sizes too large for it, the figure shuffled toward Julia's tiny Volkswagen. As it drew nearer, she could clearly see that the figure was a man, but no man like she'd ever known. He resembled less a human than one of Easter Island's famous Moai, so extraordinarily massive was his head in relation to his body. Startled by the appearance of this midnight trespasser, Julia instinctively locked her doors. She honked her car's horn in an effort to frighten the man, but he continued shuffling forward, his head seemingly expanding with every step. "It must be one," he repeated, louder and louder as he advanced. "It must be one." Julia, not wanting to run over the elongated man but also not willing to exit her car with him so close, shifted into reverse and pulled back onto the road. She drove to a friend's house and spent the night there. The next morning, she found no trace of the man in her driveway or anywhere near her home.

Similar encounters with the wobbly people proliferated throughout our town in subsequent weeks. The collected tales dealing with the wobbly people were outlandish and bizarre and seemed to hold no meaning, but they became so ubiquitous that we couldn't ignore them. Even if we managed to avoid contact with the wobbly people ourselves, many of our friends and relatives hadn't. We all knew someone who had seen the wobbly people, someone we trusted to tell the unvarnished truth. Though it pained us, we were forced to reckon with the fact that the knock on Danielle Cinder's door had clearly not been an isolated incident.

In response, we gathered our friends and our family and our co-workers and our casual acquaintances—anyone who lived in the town and might be willing to join hands—and held weekly meetings where we discussed "the wobbly invasion." At those meetings, we debated the possible origins and motivations of the wobbly people and the details of proper home security we might deploy against them. We presented potential methods of protecting the jelly and lectured one another on the efficacy of neighborhood watches. We looked into installing electric fences and barred windows across our entire town. We considered buying baseball bats and handguns and bear mace in wholesale quantities. We read about self-defense techniques online and tried to demonstrate those techniques—often poorly and incorrectly—at the meetings. We made ourselves feel that we were dealing with the situation even if, in reality, we never leapt the gorge between discussion and action.

The base problem was that we simply couldn't bring ourselves to confront the wobbly people. Something about coming face to face with them liquefied our innards, corroded whatever steely resolve we thought we might have possessed. It was as if the wobbly people twisted nerves we didn't even realize were a part of ourselves, nerves that stretched from our insular lives to the incepting spark of human consciousness.

Unhappy with our own efforts in dealing with the wobbly people, we turned to the jelly for defensive support. We studied its embedded, glimmering shards for intelligible patterns of refracted light, for coded signals, for any form of direction or knowledge. We wrote questions on slips of paper and rolled them into scrolls that we inserted into the jelly, hoping that when we retrieved them later, they might include answers. But the jelly remained silent. It kept its secrets hidden, leaving us to scrabble for security in mounting confusion and dread.

We didn't lose our trust in the jelly then—not exactly—but its implacability did raise questions. Why, we wondered, would the jelly choose us as its caretakers and our town as its resting place only to abandon us to whatever fate the wobbly people had in store? Why would it fall into our laps only to be stripped from us later? Were we wrong in thinking the wobbly people had arrived to steal away the jelly? What else could they possibly want, if not that? And perhaps most pressing, what would happen to us if, with our backs against the wall, we didn't surrender the jelly at all?

The Disappearances

On a calm, cloudless night not quite two months after the first wobbly visit, all the contactees vanished. Danielle Cinder and her son, Stanley Hillson, Julia Esparanza, and every other person in every other household that had received a visit from the wobbly people simply disappeared from our town and, as far as we have been able to determine, the entire world.

We found out about the disappearances only gradually, as certain friends failed to return our texts, certain co-workers didn't show up to important meetings, and certain businesses we patronized never again opened their doors. Children went uncharacteristically absent from classes and daycares. Appointments with doctors and dentists and mechanics and plumbers went broken. Shifts at many a minimum-wage job went unstaffed.

Our town, already fading into uneasy spectrality, discovered half its population blown away like a thin, morning mist.

As any rational people might, those of us who remained began to search for the missing. We visited their homes, picking locks on back doors and breaking windows to gain entrance when we received no responses to our bellowed "Hellos" or our frenzied ringing of doorbells. We understood the illegality of our actions but felt that investigations by police from outside our town might jeopardize the jelly's prized secrecy and sanctity.

Within the houses of the vanished we uncovered scant evidence of wrongdoing. No toppled chairs or smashed vases greeted our sleuthing eyes. No blood-stained knives or smoking guns lay in guilt on the houses' terrazzo floors. Full compliments of clothes hung in neat order within closets; jewelry nestled snug and undisturbed in its boxes. Cell phones—all mysteriously fully charged—rested unbroken on bedside tables and couch arms and kitchen counters. If violence had ever infiltrated these domiciles, it had been so sudden and so futile that it hadn't left a trace of its mayhem.

Although we may not have discovered telltale signs of crime, we did note two consistent features in the contactees' houses. First, every last drop of jelly was also missing—an unusual fact considering that the expensive and ornate vessels that had held it mere days before still glittered on coffee tables and mantelpieces. When we ran our fingers over the concavities of the containers, they came away without the slightest residue, as though they had been scrubbed clean or never used to cradle the jelly at all. Second, within each house we found several puddles of a slick, colorless liquid on floor—puddles that, no matter how often we sopped them up with towels, reformed in the same locations. Some of us claimed that the number of puddles in each house was equal to the number of its vanished inhabitants, but most of us willfully ignored any mathematical correlation, too unnerved by the panorama of eldritch implications such correlation would have painted upon our minds.

Beyond these two eccentricities, we unearthed no clues. We dredged nearby swamps for bodies. We scoured our jagged beachheads for footprints or campsites. We staked out motels and hotels to see if we might catch our kith and kin checking in or out. But we found nothing. Much as we wanted to play the part, we were not detectives. Our anemic powers of observation and deduction brought us no closer to finding our friends, our family, and our neighbors. And still we refused to contact authorities with more experience and resources. Call it pride or paranoia or a conditioned response to shrink from the outside world, but we couldn't allow our vanished townsfolk to be sought out by anyone but ourselves. The problem was ours and ours alone.

So, we searched, and we waited, and we hoped that we might see a miraculous sign to lead us toward reunification. And all the while, as we yearned for the impossible, something entirely unexpected drifted into our town to take our missing population's place—something that carried with it our final, irresolvable dissolution.

The Madness

In the weeks that followed the disappearances, sightings of the wobbly people slowed to a trickle. When we did spot them, they were always at a distance, always on the peripheral of our vision. Rather than wobbling closer to us, they held back, perhaps watching for our further responses, perhaps biding their time for future actions we could not remotely guess at. As far as we could tell, they didn't attempt to contact any more of us, either. The general scuttlebutt about town included no anecdotes concerning the peal of plaintive voices in the night or the pounding of doors by elongated hands. Even our phones continued to function in a relatively normal, unimpeded way.

That the threat posed by the wobbly people seemed to be diminishing should have brought us at least a partial sense of relief. But as the wobbly people drew themselves into the horizon, we felt only bitter unease. Their subtle retreat—if retreat it was—made no sense. If they had been responsible for the disappearances, then why not take the rest of us? If they had the power to vanish half a town without raising an alarm, why didn't they abscond with the entirety of the jelly long ago and leave us in peace? And, most alarmingly, if they were well and truly finished with us, why did they still lurk at the edges of our lives? These were the questions that howled through the canyons of our minds as we tried to work, the thoughts that propped open our eyelids as we tried to sleep.

Day in and day out, an unnamable anxiety bored its way into us. We began to miss work regularly, though many of us had no paid leave left to use. We pulled our children out of school without any plan for their future education. We boarded up our windows and installed extra locks on our doors, stocked up on canned goods and stored extra gasoline in our garages. At night, we turned off our lights and lit candles to see by. We sat with our backs to our walls, our thumbs stroking steak knife handles and the claw end of hammers. In the dim glow of our homes, we read survival manuals to our children, our pets, ourselves.

From an outsider's perspective, it would've seemed that we were preparing for a hurricane or a blizzard or the end of the world. In a way, maybe that was exactly what we *were* doing. Maybe that was what we'd been doing for a long time. Apocalypses come in many sizes, shapes, and lengths, after all. Yes, perhaps that was precisely it. Apocalypse had found us, and it found us in the most unexpected way, for, as we hunkered down inside our homes, somehow exploring new depths to our solitude, something revelatory began to happen: the jelly began to talk to us.

That term isn't quite right, though. It didn't so much "talk" as beam ideas and images directly into our neural networks via the candlelight reflected and refracted in its sparkling flecks.

While we huddled in shadow and near-silence, the glint of transmuted flame sliced through our eyes and showed us all manner of cryptic things: a mechanism that resembled a starburst constructed from hundreds of ever-lengthening corkscrews, a creature comprised of dozens of distinct anthropoid appendages without a physical trunk, a whirlpool of eyes with x-shaped pupils spiraling endlessly outward from a pinpoint of absolute emptiness. These were but a tiny smattering of the images the jelly fired across our brainpans.

The ideas it conveyed to us baffled us even further. It "told" us many things: that the sum of all possible mathematical equations is zero, that time is a psychosis brought on by biochemical processes, and that the shape of the universe is not a geometric figure, but a sound. It also "told" us that the human body is a catastrophe of biological engineering, but, through a multistep process beginning with the removal of all muscle and bone, it could be perfected.

Even if we didn't follow that particular transformative instruction (which several of us did—to horrifying and largely dire results), many of us still found ourselves altered by the jelly's messages. Trapped between the specter of the wobbly people and the jelly's psychic flood, we had nowhere to run, nowhere to turn for sanctuary. Hunched in the dank corners of our homes all hours of the night and day, we scribbled out the "thoughts" the jelly conveyed to us on any surface we could find. At first, we tried to record the messages electronically, in our computers and our phones, but these documents refused to be saved so prosaically, returning error messages of every brand when we attempted to upload them to cloud storage or house them in our own hard drives.

In lieu of high technology, we ordered notebooks and tablets and thousands of reams of paper upon which to enshrine the jelly's thoughts, but we discovered we filled these too quickly to maintain a constant stock. As a result, we gradually inscribed our walls and our floors and our ceilings with the gospel of the jelly, and when those spaces grew too crowded to be of use, we carved the thoughts into our arms, our legs, our chests and stomachs and faces. Our every patch of flesh we offered as parchment, our ever drop of blood we offered as ink. We scarred ourselves in the name of the jelly and the messages we felt must surely constitute supreme wisdom. And, as time progressed, we grew pleased with our work. We grew important and righteous, like prophets of old. You might even say, in a sense, we grew complete.

The Final Cost

Now, with half our population missing and many of us deep in the throes of mania, there is little left to speak of as "our town."

Our downtown, where once, not so very long ago, we had gathered to celebrate ourselves and our independence, sits untended. Weeds and grasses choke its sidewalks. Businesses and homes along its streets emit no welcoming light. The bronze seal we erected in the town square lies collapsed and corroded, an object of vandalism or shoddy construction we will never know.

As for ourselves, we work when we must, and we deal with outsiders when it cannot be otherwise helped. Occasionally investigators will show up, seeking missing persons on behalf of concerned relatives or angry creditors, and, in those situations, we provide the requisite amount of interest and information to quell suspicions. Mainly, though, we hide ourselves away in our houses, transcribing the word of the jelly to the best of our abilities and swimming in sheaves of paper. When our paper runs low, we continue to write, cutting script into ever-deepening layers of ourselves. Some of us have struck muscle and scrimshawed our own bones. Some of us have begun to wonder whether our vital organs might be capable of holding a few select epigraphs. And some of us have even eyed our children's blank flesh, so desperate for new surfaces upon which to enshrine the jelly's message.

It's easy to call our actions insane. It's easy to point a finger and say, "the isolation drove them crazy" or "their obsession with the outré overwhelmed them." But how mad are we, really? The jelly talks to us, and to us alone. It has torn us apart and opened our doors to strange, wobbly terrors, but it has also accepted us as its own. We have greater purpose than ever before. We stand more united in one cause than at any other point in our history. And, above all else, we have finally earned validation—not from ourselves or a competing backwater community or the urbanites of a middling metropolis, but from the cosmos itself. How could a people—any people—ask for more than that?

ACKNOWLEDGMENTS

Huge thanks go out to Jon Padgett and Grimscribe Press. Without Jon's hard work and belief in this collection and my writing in general, it would've never come into being. Thanks to all the amazing editors and publishers who have stood by my work over the years, including but not limited to Sam Cowan and Justin Steele, Wendy Wagner and John Joseph Adams, Michael Kelly, Steve Berman, Robert Wilson, C.C. Finlay, Matt Edginton, and Jordan Krall. Thanks to the many writers who inspire me and who are far too numerous to list. Eternal gratitude to my family, especially Erin and Malcolm, for giving me everything, ever. And always, always, thank you to my readers. Without you, I would be nothing but a lone voice screaming to itself in the darkness.

ABOUT THE AUTHOR

Kurt Fawver is a writer of horror, weird fiction, and literature that oozes through the cracks of genre. His short fiction has won a Shirley Jackson Award and been previously published in venues such as *The Magazine of Fantasy & Science Fiction*, *Strange Aeons*, *Weird Tales*, *Vastarien*, *Best New Horror*, and *Year's Best Weird Fiction*. He's the author of two collections of short stories-*The Dissolution of Small Worlds* (Lethe Press) and *Forever, in Pieces* (Villipede Publications. He's also had non-fiction published in journals such as *Thinking Horror* and the *Journal of the Fantastic in the Arts*.

GRIMSCRIBE PRESS

www.ingramcontent.com/pod-product-compliance
Lightning Source LLC
LaVergne TN
LVHW041802060526
838201LV00046B/1102
* 9 7 9 8 2 1 8 0 3 9 5 8 5 *